"Damn, you've got a great butt."

On all fours, Mallory gave Jack a "come hither" look over her shoulder. "And what do you want to do to it, Jack?"

His surprised gaze flicked to her face. "As in?"

She reached back and gave an experimental smack to her left cheek. "Do you want to spank it? After all, I've been a very naughty girl."

And she *had* been naughty. Jack clearly wanted more out of their relationship, yet she had told him that as far as she was concerned their relationship was nothing more than sex. Even though she knew that wasn't entirely true.

She heard his low, primal growl as he knelt on the bed behind her. "I don't know…do you want to be spanked?" he rasped.

"I might be interested in a love tap or two." Mallory wiggled her bottom and he grasped her hip, his fingers denting her flesh.

She felt a light, stinging smack to her right cheek and gasped.

"Hold still, then, naughty girl, and take your punishment," he said wickedly. "But don't worry. I promise I'll kiss it all better…."

Dear Reader,

Sugar 'n spice and everything naughty has been the theme of the first two books in our KISS & TELL miniseries, and we see no reason to stop now! Not when the two remaining characters, Mallory Woodruff and Jack Daniels, have been indulging in some, um, under the covers activity without telling their friends...or anyone else!

In *Just Between Us...* documentary producer Mallory Woodruff figures she has the best of both worlds when she and newspaper columnist Jack Daniels become lovers. But when Jack suggests they let the world in on their little secret, Mallory balks, making him feel as if he's being used simply for sex. What happens when he refuses to give her what she so desires? The battle of the sexes has never been so hot....

We hope you enjoy Mallory and Jack's sassy adventure! We'd love to hear what you think. Write to us at P.O. Box 12271, Toledo, OH 43612 (we'll respond with a signed bookplate, newsletter and bookmark) or visit us on the Web at www.toricarrington.com for fun drawings.

Here's wishing you love, romance and happy reading.

Lori & Tony Karayianni
aka Tori Carrington

Books by Tori Carrington

JUST BETWEEN US...

Tori Carrington

HARLEQUIN®

TORONTO • NEW YORK • LONDON
AMSTERDAM • PARIS • SYDNEY • HAMBURG
STOCKHOLM • ATHENS • TOKYO • MILAN • MADRID
PRAGUE • WARSAW • BUDAPEST • AUCKLAND

We wholeheartedly dedicate this book
to our fellow dreamers:

Those who dream by night in the dusty recesses of their mind wake in the morning to find that it was vanity. But the dreamers of the day are dangerous people, for they dream their dreams with open eyes, and make them come true.
—*T. E. Lawrence*

ISBN 0-373-79117-8

JUST BETWEEN US...

Copyright © 2003 by Lori and Tony Karayianni.

1

"...THE BIGGER THE BUDGET, the better the bang. Or so this reporter believed until I recently viewed a documentary by up-and-coming producer Mallory Woodruff on the U.S./Mexico border war. I, personally, look forward to more from this talented filmmaker. Just think what she could do with a real budget!"

Oh, I don't know, Mallory Woodruff thought caustically as she downed her second cup of coffee. *Pay my rent, maybe?*

She refolded the paper and sat back in the bar-style, high-backed chair in the freshly painted new home of her best friend's pastry shop, Sugar 'n' Spice. It might be eight o'clock, but she'd need either a whole lot more time, or at least three more cups of Reilly's coffee to wake up.

"So?"

Mallory blinked Reilly's pretty face into focus. Or rather tried to. When Layla, another one of their circle of four friends, had woken her from the dead a half hour ago, she'd been afraid something had happened to one of them. In a town where the word "friend" was thrown around with careless abandon, she'd been relieved to find Reilly Chudowski, Layla Hollister and Jack Daniels were the real thing when their paths had crossed three years ago.

But she was veering off course, wasn't she? The reason she was sitting at a front corner table that overlooked Wilshire Boulevard, when she'd rather be sleeping off the previous night's pitcher of homemade margaritas, was that Layla had mentioned an emergency. Considering that Layla was marrying hottie ex-plastic surgeon Sam Lovejoy tomorrow, well, she figured just about anything could qualify.

Anything but what she'd just read in the *Hollywood Confidential.*

"So...what?" Mallory grumbled. "This half a breath meets the criteria for an emergency meeting?"

Layla and Reilly stared at her, looking extraordinarily stunned, while Jack grimaced, unsurprised, and shook his head.

"Is nothing capable of impressing you?" Reilly asked, apparently more than a bit put out.

"Sure." Mallory reached across the table and took the rest of Layla's half-eaten sticky bun. "You guys impress me all the time." She slanted a glance at Jack as she stuck the sweet into her mouth to calm her roaring stomach. "With the exception of you, of course, Jack. You need to find yourself a goal."

Jack had to be the most attractive man she'd ever laid eyes on. He was Brad Pitt, Robert Redford and George Clooney all wrapped up into one scrumptious package.

Of course, she wished he had the ambition of a drive-thru server.

Jack snatched the paper from her hands. "Hey, I was using that to catch the crumbs," she protested with a smile.

"You stick so much into your mouth there aren't any crumbs," he grumbled back.

Reilly leaned her elbows on the table. "But doesn't that piece mean you might catch the attention of a major studio? Get that budget the reporter mentioned?"

Mallory made a face and stole Jack's napkin to clean syrup off her hands. "First off, it's not a piece, it's a mention. And in a word—no."

Layla sighed. "God, you can be so negative sometimes."

Mallory waved her away even though the comment stung, a little bit anyway. She was a realist, not a pessimist. And the reality was that documentary producers spent the majority of their time applying and interviewing for grants and scrounging for financing and had more sense than to bask in the glow of a few throwaway comments that would reap absolutely zero results.

Of course, it didn't help her attitude that she was having major problems raising the money she needed to work on her current documentary about the infamous murder twenty-five years ago of a young actress called The Red Gardenia. Forget her rent. Yesterday her cameraman had threatened to walk out on her if she didn't pay what she owed him for the past month.

She scratched the back of her neck. Then there was that little time limit she'd given herself when she'd first come to L.A. Five years. She'd given herself five years to make it in the city. And obviously she hadn't made it yet. And that five-year anniversary mark was coming up quickly. Too quickly.

But she wasn't going to tell Layla that. To do so would be to focus on the negative. Today presented a whole slew of fresh opportunities. And that's where she preferred to concentrate her energies: the future and all its possibilities.

Well, on that and taking an easy jab at her friend.

"Shouldn't you be off gaping down someone's throat or up someone's colon, Dr. Hollister?" she asked.

Reilly barked with laughter, then caught herself when Layla stared at her. "Hey, it was funny."

Layla took her purse from the back of her seat

and hiked the strap over her shoulder. "I'm off from the clinic until the New Year. Remember?"

"Ah. Then I amend my previous comment. Both you and Jack need to find some ambition."

"I have ambition."

Mallory hiked a brow. "Getting married isn't an ambition, Lay. It's death."

Jack mumbled something under his breath and pushed from the table. "I need a refill."

"Get me one, too," Mallory called after him.

Reilly and Layla shared a stare then looked at her.

"Does Jack seem a bit grumpier than usual?" Layla asked.

Mallory scratched her nose. "Not that I've noticed."

"I think he is, too," Reilly said to Layla.

Mallory shrugged. "Maybe he has a column due or something."

Layla shook her head. "No…no. It's something more than that. I can tell. Something's bothering him."

"I'm sure he's fine," Mallory said. "He's always fine."

Which was an out and out lie. Because she *had* noticed that Jack seemed particularly irritable and irritating lately. But to admit that might require her also to admit that she knew because when Layla had called he'd been lying in bed next to her with one of his legs covering hers and his hand over her right breast. And she couldn't do that. Namely because Reilly and Layla would kill her if they ever found out she'd gone back on the promise they'd made three years ago for the three of them to maintain a platonic relationship with the ultra-yummy Jack Daniels. Keep the friendship, ax the sexual complications.

Well, she had kept the promise. For about six hours. Before she'd ripped off his clothes and indulged in fantasies she hadn't even known she'd fostered.

Mallory cleared her throat. Of course, it had only happened the one night. Well, okay, it had happened another night about three months after that. Then every couple months like clockwork she and Jack would end up taking a wicked tumble. Up until three months ago, anyway. Since then they were either at his place or hers three or four times a week.

But if Layla and Reilly ever found out...

"Remember, I need you guys there by six," Layla said, getting up from her chair.

Mallory blinked at her. "Need us where?"

"The rehearsal dinner."

"Oh, yeah. Right." Mallory pointed at her. "I'll be there."

Layla narrowed her eyes. "You'd better be, Mall. The last thing I need is to have to worry about you."

"Hey, I said I'll be there, so I'll be there."

Jack came back to the table and handed out fresh cups of coffee. "I'll make sure she gets there on time."

Layla's face instantly relaxed. "Thanks, Jack."

Mallory sighed. "Why is it when he says anything, you guys accept it like it's the God-spoken truth, but you question everything that comes out of my mouth?"

Reilly smiled at her. "Not everything. Only those things associated with events you'd rather not attend."

"Like my engagement party," Layla said.

"Or my reopening two weeks ago," Reilly pointed out.

"You guys didn't need me at either place."

"No," Layla said, "but we wanted you there."

It was nice, Mallory thought, how these guys needed her, even if sometimes it was a little suffocating. Didn't they understand that she was used to looking after herself and only herself? That growing up she'd been so much extra luggage that her mother probably wouldn't have filled in the lost baggage form at the airport should Mallory have gotten misplaced en route to her latest husband's apartment/house/condo?

Of course they didn't understand. Because she'd never really told them about life growing up as Mallory Woodruff. Because to do so would be to dredge up the past. And there was that thing about her liking only to look out on to the future.

"Sorry," she said blithely.

They laughed.

"Okay, maybe that could have sounded a little more sincere," she admitted. "But the sentiments are there. The last thing I want to do is hurt any of you."

Layla leaned over and gave her a hug. "Now that sounded more genuine."

Even Jack seemed to be looking at her a little too closely. Mallory reached across for his last sticky bun. He moved it out of reach.

Layla smiled. "I'll see you guys at six. On the dot. Not a minute earlier, not a minute later."

Mallory gave her a military salute, which, she supposed, was apropos given what she wore: fatigues, short black boots and T-shirt that read Three Stages Of Marriage: Lust, Rust And Die. "Yes, sir. I mean, ma'am."

"I'm going to make you pay for that one," Layla said.

Considering all that was going on over the next day and a half, Mallory had little doubt that she would.

TWELVE HOURS LATER at Layla and Sam's rehearsal dinner Jack watched Mallory as if it were the first time he'd seen her. The woman had absolutely no clue how he really felt about her. Of course, it prob-ably didn't help that whenever they were around Layla and Reilly he had to be so careful to keep his expression neutral. He watched the way Mall's mouth moved when she talked and wondered why it was he always wanted to kiss her when she was speaking.

For a moment there, the briefest of moments, the agitation he'd been feeling lately dropped away and he was able to enjoy Mallory the woman. For a moment there, she'd emerged something other than the driven, career-minded producer. She'd even seemed a bit human, somehow.

Then the moment had passed and he was left star-ing at a sexy, dynamic woman he wanted more than any other woman he'd ever met.

A woman who was beginning to irritate him to no end.

That wasn't normal, was it? Was it possible to want to have sex with someone yet want to kill them at the same time?

"I feel naked," Mallory was saying to Layla's stepmother—who looked younger than Layla and not a fraction as smart.

Jack's gaze took in the simple black slacks and vest Mallory had on. Definitely not naked. But def-initely not her usual attire of jeans and a T-shirt bearing an offensive saying on the front, either. How Mallory would ever make it through tonight and tomorrow without being able to express her emotions through her clothes loomed an unanswered question.

Of course Sharon Hollister wore little more than lingerie by way of a pink slip dress, which meant it was unlikely she'd get where Mallory was coming from. For all intents and purposes, Sharon might as well be naked.

Hmm... Jack wondered how much he'd have to pay Mallory to wear one of those dresses....

"If you'll excuse me, I think my husband's motioning for me to rejoin him," the trophy wife with the artificially enhanced lips and unnaturally plump, unmarked brow line said politely. Then she made a beeline for anywhere away from Mallory.

Jack looked over the exclusive room at the Beverly Hills Wilshire Hotel that the Hollisters had reserved for the occasion. In his monthly columns he often criticized the extravagant spending and monetary excesses of the rich, mostly because he had witnessed countless examples of it growing up in the wealthy Daniels family. But he didn't think Layla would forgive him if he shined his light on her father and stepmother's desire to dump the annual income of five families into one wedding occasion. Lord knew Layla hadn't wanted the spectacle. She and Sam had wanted to take off to Vegas for a five-minute quickie wedding in front of an Elvis impersonator.

He looked over to one side of the palm-decorated room, which held just the right amount of tasteful holiday decorations without going overboard. There, Layla talked to what he knew was her real mother, who looked about as comfortable in her surroundings as Mallory purportedly felt. He noticed Mall yet again perform a shimmy, trying to get comfortable in her clothes, and then he took in the other twenty guests. It struck him that no one would miss him and Mallory. If only for a few precious minutes.

He leaned backward and cracked open the door to the service hall. Everyone had already eaten, the rehearsal with the minister had gone off without a hitch, and aside from the female bartender manning the open bar across the room, there wasn't a single service person in sight.

Jack grasped Mall's wrist and yanked her back into the corridor with him.

She gasped, instantly trying to break free. "Are you insane?" she demanded, her dark hair curling wildly around her round, kissable face, her light brown eyes almost yellow as they flashed fire at him. Enough fire that he knew she was as turned on as he was by the possibilities their solitude presented. "They'll see us for sure."

"So we'll tell them I needed a cigarette and you came out to keep me company."

She narrowed her eyes and licked her lips in telltale anticipation as he tugged her down the corridor, found a linen closet, then pulled her inside and closed the door.

Being Mallory Woodruff's lover usually took a lot of invention and a whole lot of stick-to-itness. Unless she was the initiator, that is. Then all bets were off. All he had to do was hold on for one helluva ride.

Jack looked around for the switch to turn off the light but couldn't find one.

Mallory didn't seem to mind as she yanked her vest over her head then started on her slacks. "God, I've been itching to get out of these things all night."

Oh, yeah. But unfortunately she'd have to put them back on way too soon.

When she finally stood in front of Jack wearing nothing but a pair of black panties and bra, he chuckled. It seemed Mallory had managed to get her point across through her clothes. Only tonight she'd done so by way of her naughty black panties. Across the satiny front they read Bite Me.

He gripped her hips and hauled her to him. Biting her was exactly what he planned to do. For starters.

"You're not getting undressed," she complained as her hands slid over his rear through his slacks then snaked around front to dive into the waist.

"One of us should try to stay as undisheveled as possible."

"Oh, yeah?" she asked, rerouting her hands to his hair where she proceeded to ruffle the hell out of it. "Explain how a cigarette did that," she murmured before plastering her full, juicy mouth against his and kissing him like a woman bent on destruction.

"The wind." Jack worked his fingers under the elastic at the back of her panties until he firmly cupped her sweet flesh.

Mallory was at least a foot shorter than he was, which had proven a challenge in the beginning, but was something he barely noticed now. When they were lying in bed, height didn't matter.

Now, however, with both of them standing and no available object around to help level the playing field, he felt a crick building at the back of his neck already. As she licked his neck and pressed her womanhood full throttle against him, he also felt on fire with need.

"We've got to hurry," she rasped, unfastening the front of his pants and freeing his rock-hard arousal.

Jack stretched his neck and clamped his teeth together as her fingers encircled him. No matter how many times he felt her touch, it was like the first time all over again. It never failed to amaze him how much control this one little spitfire had over him. He'd wanted her every second of every day for three years. In the beginning, he'd been successful at staving off his attraction to her. At least to some extent. Now he was as much a slave to it as he had once been to drink.

Addictive personality disorder. That's what an overpaid shrink had told him when he was nineteen, in college, and drunk more than he was sober. In a life where he could rely on few things—his jet-setting parents had been too busy with their social life and traveling around the world for him to form any meaningful bond with them—the whiskey bottle had always been there. Empty? No problem. Twenty bucks bought him another one.

But with Mallory…

With Mallory he felt constantly like a guy staring at an empty bottle wanting more. Except at moments like this. When he could feel her nipples pressing into the middle of his palms. Hear her rapid breathing and whispered orders in his ears. Sense the urgency in her as his own reached a feverish pitch.

Mallory's fingers squeezed his shaft almost to the point of pain then moved up and down.

He'd have to bite her later.…

"Hold onto my shoulders," he ground out, running his hands over her outer thighs then lifting her so her legs hugged his hips. He immediately felt her damp heat against his straining erection and groaned.

"Condom," he said. "Back right—"

"Pocket," she finished, waving the foil packet at him.

She opened it with her teeth, then within two blinks had him sheathed and beyond ready.

Only the position wasn't as easy as it seemed.

"Back me up," she said sharply, growing as frustrated as he was.

You would think that they hadn't had sex for six weeks instead of just that morning.

"You're a bossy woman, you know that?"

She smiled, her eyes darkening as she stared at his mouth. "I know." She kissed him. "Do it."

He did it.

The moment her back met with the smooth wood of the door, she slapped her hands against it, using the barrier to steady herself. He looked down to find her at an accessible angle, her engorged flesh blossoming open and waiting to be claimed.

Dear Lord in heaven, but what this woman did to him.

Jack grasped her hips and fit the knob of his arousal against her tight opening, then stayed there, allowing sweet anticipation to wash over him. This was his whiskey bottle now. Mallory. And this instant right before…

Mallory bucked her hips forward and forced entry, then slid all the way down until her pelvis met fully with his.

Her moan mingled with his groan.

Oh, yes...

"Oh, no," Mallory whispered, her eyes as big as the dessert plates in the other room.

2

MALLORY SWALLOWED HARD. It wasn't possible that... There was no way that...

The door to the linen closet vibrated again.

"Hello?" a female voice drifted through the wood. "Is somebody in there?"

"Oh God," Mallory whispered. "Oh God, oh God, oh God."

She moved to put her legs down.

Jack only gripped her tighter.

"Jack, I—" She breathed.

He put a finger over her lips, a decidedly wicked look in his mocha-brown eyes. "Shh."

He moved inside her. One long stroke that made a moan gather at the back of her throat, leaving her mouth eager to let it loose.

He wasn't... He didn't...

He stroked her again, long, hard and deep and her ability to think stopped altogether.

She didn't care if both Layla and Reilly were standing on the other side of that door. She didn't care if the L.A. police were about to break it in. All she could concentrate on was how very good it felt to have Jack so deep inside her.

"Oooh, oooh, oooh!" she rasped, trying to gain purchase against the moving door even as her crisis built.

"That's it," Jack said, leaning in to suckle her neck. "Come for me."

And she did.

Her orgasm seemed to stretch on and on and on even as Jack stilled and strained in the throes of his own climax.

After long, heart-pounding moments Mallory blinked open her eyes to stare at the man who had given her more mind-blowing orgasms than any ten men combined. It wasn't even remotely possible that every time just kept getting better and better, was it?

"Hello?" the voice drifted through the wood again along with a loud knock. "Open the door right this instant."

Mallory swallowed hard as Jack finally allowed her to slide down his length to stand. Her body shivered at the sensation while her mind slowly grasped the levity of the situation.

Layla and Reilly were going to kill her.

She groaned as she stepped into her panties and slacks and tried to find the way back into her vest. "What are we going to say?" she whispered fiercely to Jack, who was putting himself together with one hand while he held the door closed with the other.

She stared at him as he stared back.

"Why not the truth?"

Mallory's throat closed off air altogether. He wasn't seriously considering telling them that they'd been sleeping together, was he?

"Are you insane?" she asked.

"Shh."

She realized she'd nearly shouted the words.

Jack turned so that his back rested against the wood separating them from the persistent person on the other side of the door. He crossed his arms over his broad and impressive chest, looking a little too cheeky for her liking. "Actually, I've been thinking about this for a while and I think it's about time we let them in on our little secret."

Mallory's movements slowed as she turned the vest right side out then yanked it over her head. "Okay, it's official. You are insane."

"Why?"

She straightened her top then went to work on her hair. "Come on, Jack. We've talked about this. Whatever happened to 'what they don't know won't hurt them'?"

"That's always been your take on the situation."

She squinted at him, trying to reconcile the man she'd known just a few minutes before with the man he was introducing her to now. "And *your* take?"

She figured she was as fixed up as she was going to get and folded her own arms over her chest, facing off with him.

"My take is that I'd like to let our friends—our best friends—know that we're seeing each other."

Mallory nearly toppled over. "Seeing each other? Jack, what we do is not seeing each other. What we do is have...sex."

Was it her, or had he just winced?

She uncrossed her arms and gestured wildly with her hands. "I mean, to be seeing each other, we'd actually have to date. And we don't date. We've never dated. You've never called me up and said 'Hey, what's say we catch a movie.'"

"I bring over DVDs."

"And that constitutes a relationship? We don't even get around to watching the damn movies 'cause we're too busy having sex."

Again, a wince.

Oh, no. This was not happening.

Mallory reached around him for the door handle. She needed to get out of this room but quick. She wondered if it was possible for claustrophobia to lie dormant then just spring out and overwhelm the victim in a single moment. "We'll tell them I...spilled wine or something on my vest and you were helping me find something to clean it up with. And...and... the door got jammed."

"And what? I blew on the spot until it dried and went away?" Jack stayed put, refusing her exit.

She stared up into his eyes. His deep, dark, wonderful eyes that were now looking at her as if she'd just committed some heinous crime.

"What?" she asked, growing increasingly frustrated with his inexplicable behavior.

And feeling increasingly claustrophobic.

He shrugged his shoulders, his arms still crossed. "It's simple, Mall. If we don't tell Layla and Reilly, and I mean come clean with everything, then our relationship—excuse me, the sex—ends right here."

Mallory's jaw dropped open. "You...can't...be... serious."

He nodded soberly. "As serious as I've ever been in my life."

"Hello!" the voice in the hall grew louder.

If there was one thing Mallory had never responded well to, it was ultimatums. She'd grown up with her mother saying, "Mallory Marie, behave or I'll send you to live with your grandmother in Portland." And lately everyone seemed to be throwing around ultimatums. "Pay up your rent or you're out," her landlord had told her last week. "Pay me last month's salary or I quit," her cameraman had said. "Our foundation needs to have final approval or we don't grant you the money," she'd heard just this morning when she was pounding the pavement trying to scare up the money for the cameraman's salary.

But none of the other ultimatums had made her feel like she might be sick. Standing there looking at Jack, and knowing he was serious, made her heart ache in a way that frightened her.

Despite his words, he couldn't be serious. He couldn't be. She didn't have time for a relationship. She didn't know where she was career-wise. She'd been in L.A. for nearly five years but didn't know yet if she had what it took to make it in the dog-eat-dog city. Things had worked so well between them the way they were. And now Jack wanted to change everything.

God, Jack Daniels wasn't even her type.

She caught the ridiculous thought. She didn't have a type. But if she did, Jack Daniels would fit the criteria to a T.

Another round of pounding. "I'm going to get security!"

Mallory cleared her throat. She didn't know what else to say, so she said the obvious. "She's going to get security."

Jack stared at her for a long minute. "That's your answer?"

Mallory's fear-o-meter shot up another notch. "What? That she's going to get security?"

"Mmm."

"Then, yes," she nodded inanely. "That's my

answer. Because…because…because your question is irrelevant, Jack.''

Her response seemed to stun him enough to allow her to maneuver him out of the way of the door.

She opened it to find that neither Layla nor Reilly were standing outside, nor anyone they knew for that matter. Rather, a woman who was obviously part of the hotel staff looked more than a little hot and bothered that she hadn't been able to get into the room.

"Excuse me," Mallory said, pushing past her before the woman could say anything.

Of course, if her need to get out of there quick had anything to do with the tears pricking the back of her eyelids, well, she wasn't admitting anything.

WHAT A DIFFERENCE FIVE minutes made.

As Jack stood off to the side of the reception room watching the melee unfold before him, he couldn't bring himself to believe it was the same room he and Mallory had left a short time before. While everyone had been speaking civilly before, smiling, drinking and being merry (well, at least as merry as this mismatched group could get), now clear battle lines had been drawn and the bride's family and friends were going toe-to-toe with the groom's.

"It's off," Layla said, looking much as Mallory had in the linen closet as she crossed her arms over her chest and stared down her groom, Sam Lovejoy. "The wedding is officially cancelled."

Sam leaned forward, a tight grin detracting from his handsomeness not at all. "Layla, don't be ridiculous. We can work all this out after the ceremony tomorrow." He waggled his brows. "You know, on our way to our honeymoon."

Layla looked like the dentist had just told her to open wide. "Honeymoon? Honeymoon?" She poked her finger into Sam's wide chest. "I've got news for you, Dr. Lovejoy. There isn't going to be any honeymoon."

It didn't take a rocket scientist to know that something monumental had happened to bring about current events. Jack was a stickler for details. It's what made him such a good columnist.

And, he hoped, it's what would provide him with the ammo he needed to patch everything up here.

He leaned closer to Reilly where she stood next to him, looking as stunned as he felt.

"What's going on?" Jack whispered.

Reilly glanced at him. "Jesus, Jack, where have you been? World War III has broken out and you didn't even witness the first shot."

Jack resisted the urge to pull at his collar as he looked at Mallory across the room. She didn't appear to know what was going on, either, but she did look ready to jump into the fray on behalf of Layla at a moment's notice.

Jack became aware of Reilly's sharpening interest. "Where were you, anyway?"

He shoved his hands into his pants pockets as he watched Layla work to take off her diamond solitaire engagement ring. "Bathroom. What's going on?"

Someone—one of Layla's cousins, he thought—turned to shush them. Reilly ignored her and stepped closer to whisper into his ear. "Remember how Sam used to be Mr. L.A. Chop Doc? The crème de la crème of plastic surgeons?"

Jack nodded. "Yes. Then he took on the position of staff administrator at Trident Medical Group where Layla works."

"Mmm. Well, it seems he doesn't much like firing people so he told Layla tonight that when they get back from their honeymoon he's going to reopen his personal practice."

Jack grimaced. "Ouch."

"You can say that again. I don't think Layla's quite accepted yet that half the breasts in L.A. bear Sam's hand marks…"

Jack hiked his brows.

Reilly waved her hands. "You know what I mean. Anyway, knowing that he's going to be creating more of those perfect breasts, along with pert bottoms, sent her careening over the edge."

Jack rubbed his chin with his index finger. From what he understood, Layla's self-esteem when it came to body image had suffered greatly in the initial stages of her relationship with Sam. Throw in that she subscribed to the notion that medicine should be available to everybody, while Sam's personal motto was "let them have breasts," and, well, you had a tenuous situation at best.

But ultimately they had worked everything out.

Or so he'd thought.

He took in Layla and Sam bickering like a divorced couple. Had the former harmony between them existed only because Sam had given up performing plastic surgery?

Jack felt himself begin to withdraw emotionally from the situation and wishing he could do so physically. To witness this on top of what had happened with Mallory in the linen closet was a little too much excitement for one night.

Reilly quietly cleared her throat. "By the way, did I tell you that Ben and I had a falling out?"

Jack stared at her as if she'd just taken her head off then screwed it back on.

Oh, no.

That did it.

He was leaving.

Now.

Reilly was nodding. "He wants me to close down Sugar 'n' Spice and come into business with him. You know, change Benardo's Hideaway to Ben and Reilly's."

Jack suppressed the desire to say, "So?"

What was there some kind of relationship virus going around that he didn't know about?

He began doing the physical backing away he'd longed to just moments ago.

"Where are you going?" Reilly asked as Jack met Mallory's gaze across the room.

"Um, the bathroom."

Reilly looked totally confused. "But I thought you just got back from there."

He absently rubbed his churning stomach. "Yeah. Something like that." He eyed the door. "Call me when the storm clouds blow over."

Then he strode from the room as fast as he could without running.

3

"I'M SUPPOSED TO BE AT the church right now," Layla wailed over the phone to Mallory the following morning. Now that the emotional fireworks were over, apparently the bride was having second thoughts about dumping her groom.

Either that or she was mourning the dress.

"I have the image all laid out in my mind," Layla continued without any prompting from Mallory, who was hiding under the covers in her bed wishing the world and Layla would just go away. "My mother would be standing behind me fixing my veil. You'd help me put on my garter and make sure I had sexy underwear underneath, and Reilly would be calming any prewedding jitters with caffeine-free coffee and sticky buns."

Mallory's brain caught on the word coffee. She threw aside the sheet and pulled herself into a semi-standing position.

It was 10 a.m. and she was only half-awake at best. She moved her cell phone to her other ear and shuffled from her bedroom into the tiny living/dining area of her apartment, then into the closet that was her kitchen, kicking clothes, notebooks, and crumpled pieces of paper out of her way as she went. "So call Sam and patch things up," she grumbled to Layla, who was obviously heartbroken.

But at least her friend could talk about it. Mallory, on the other hand, had to keep her own relationship woes to herself.

Coffee.

She needed coffee.

She took the stained carafe out of the coffeemaker, eyed the half inch of murky contents, then dumped it down the sink.

"I can't," Layla whispered.

"Why can't you?" Mallory asked, filling the reservoir with water then taking the small coffee can from the pint-sized refrigerator. She popped the rubber top and peered inside at the grounds that barely covered the bottom of the can, then shook it. Enough for one cup. All she needed to see her through to getting to Reilly's.

"I just...can't," Layla whispered into her ear.

Mallory searched through her empty cabinet for filters and came up with nothing but a half-empty package of stale taco shells and an empty jar of peanut butter. She dropped her right hand to her side. "What's so difficult about it, Lay? All you have to do is pick up the phone, press the speed dial number for Sam, and say 'hi.'"

Layla laughed without humor. "Excuse me, but

if I'm not mistaken, you were at the dinner last night, weren't you? You saw what happened. I can't call him!''

Looked like making coffee was out.

''So don't call him then, I don't care,'' Mallory grumbled.

Silence.

Great. She'd just pissed off her grieving friend. She squinted against the sun slanting in through the kitchen window then closed the stained shade against the glare. Grieving? Layla hadn't just lost a relative. She'd called off a wedding. Purposely. With full knowledge of what she was doing.

''Filter,'' she said absently.

''What?'' Layla asked.

Mallory shook her head then trudged back out into the living room/dining room, searching for something, anything she could use as a filter. ''Nothing,'' she said. ''Look, Lay, why don't you go out somewhere? Go to Reilly's. That's where I'm planning to be in twenty minutes. Meet me there.''

A heavy sigh. ''Maybe you're right. I probably shouldn't be sitting here by myself moping around. And I've already done all the canceling that I can. By now everyone knows what happened anyway. If they don't…well, I guess they'll find out when they get to the church, won't they?''

There was a brief knock at Mallory's apartment

door. She stared at the closed and multiple-locked barrier, an image of Jack with an extra-large cup of coffee popping to mind. She wasn't sure which made her mouth water more. Jack or the coffee. She hurried to the door and threw it open.

Not Jack.

Not even coffee.

Instead, her neighbor Candy Cane stood in the doorway looking well turned out—as usual—in full makeup, teased blond hair, and pink-and-red kimono robe, likely just having returned home from a busy night walking the strip.

"Oh, it's you," Mallory said.

Candy flashed her a smile. Somewhere around forty, Candy was a prostitute who never made any apologies about who she was or what she did for a living. Mallory liked that about her.

Unfortunately she was also an early riser; something Mallory didn't like.

"Sugar?" Candy asked, dangling an empty porcelain coffee cup from one perfectly manicured finger.

"Filters?" Mallory returned.

"Who's there?" Layla asked over the phone.

"Candy. Just a second," Mallory answered then dropped the receiver to her side. "I'll trade you sugar for a coffee filter."

Candy scrunched up her nose, making her look

cuter if that were at all possible. "I don't touch the stuff. Do you know what it does to your skin?"

"I don't care what it does to my skin. I just care that it wakes me up."

Candy shook her head, walked through to the kitchen, got her sugar, then was standing in the doorway again in no time. "Thanks, hon," she said with a large smile. "And maybe you should think about some of that instant flavored stuff. I like that."

Mallory shook her own head then slammed the door after her. What kind of person didn't drink coffee?

Then again, what kind of hooker took in every kind of stray imaginable, both of the animal and human variety?

"Mallory? Mallory? Are you still there?"

Oops. Layla.

She lifted the receiver back to her ear. What had she been saying? Oh, yeah, they'd been discussing meeting up at Reilly's to help Layla make it through the day of her cancelled wedding. "I'm still here. And what you just said about everyone finding out on their own steam? Well, you sound like the Layla I know and love again already."

Mallory's gaze traveled around her apartment. Newspapers, her plastic-wrapped bridesmaid dress, the panty hose to go with it.

Panty hose…

She picked up the square package, a nagging voice at the back of her mind telling her that maybe she shouldn't. What? she answered. There was no wedding, so she didn't need them anyway.

She tore open the plastic, yanked out the silky stockings then headed back for the kitchen.

"You always make sense," Layla said. "I knew there was a reason I called you."

Mallory grimaced. Whatever that meant. She got a pair of scissors out of a drawer and cut the foot out of one of the stockings. With help from a rubber band, she fastened the makeshift filter to the holder then dumped the coffee grounds in.

"So I'll see you at Reilly's in a few, then?" Mallory asked.

"Got it," Layla confirmed.

Mallory clicked the disconnect button then put the cell down on the counter and stared as the coffeemaker gurgled then spat out her one precious cup of caffeine. Her gaze drifted back to the cell phone. She picked it up and pressed a speed dial number.

ACROSS THE WAY IN Culver City, Jack sat at his narrow kitchen table in a pair of jeans and leisurely drank a cup of coffee, his ten-year-old bloodhound at his feet, the morning newspaper in his hand. As far as apartments went, his wasn't much bigger than Mallory's. But it was much better organized. And a great deal neater. If there was one thing he hated about Mallory, it was her housekeeping skills. Or lack thereof.

No good. The negative reflection wasn't enough to chase from his mind the memory of her face as she reached orgasm in the linen closet last night.

Damn.

He glanced over the paper at the calendar on the wall with the number 26 circled in red indicating the deadline for his January column, then rustled the paper back to block it again.

What was Mallory doing right now?

He frowned. Probably sleeping. Probably thinking everything was still right as rain between them. Probably choosing to forget the entire conversation they'd had the night before.

He rustled the paper again, trying to make himself focus on the words, but he couldn't seem to link more than two of them together, and two words didn't make a sentence. Or a whole lot of sense for that matter.

Boomer lifted his head to stare at him with his droopy eyes and then whined.

"What is it, B?" Jack glanced over at the dog's full food and water bowls, then looked at the newspaper again. Boomer sighed heavily then laid his head back down.

At ten years of age—which was ancient for a bloodhound—the dog was becoming increasingly lazier. If that was even possible. One morning Jack had actually timed him and the dog hadn't moved in five straight hours. Not to eat. Not to use the dog door to go into the patch of dead grass that served as his backyard to go to the bathroom. Nothing.

He should call the vet and find out if the behavior was normal. Then again, he'd just taken Boomer to the vet for his annual two months ago and everything had checked out fine.

The only time the old hound seemed animated was when Mallory was around.

Jack gave up on the paper altogether and blew a long breath out of his inflated cheeks. If he was going to stick to his threat not to have sex with Mallory again, he'd have to stop thinking every other minute about having it with her.

The phone on the wall rang. He glanced over his shoulder where it was two feet away, then leaned back on the rear two legs of the chair to snatch up the cordless receiver.

"Yeah," he said, settling the legs of his chair back onto the floor.

"Reilly's. Quick. Pick me up."

Jack's throat tightened. It was Mallory. And she'd just said those five words.

"And bring emergency rations."

She hung up.

Jack stared at the receiver. True to form, Mallory was acting like last night had never happened.

He shut off the phone then laid it on the table.

He picked the paper back up and shook it out, this time intent on getting something out of it.

He was well into his tenth story when the phone rang again twelve minutes later.

"Are you on the road?" was Mallory's hello.

"Nope."

"Jack!" she said. "What's the matter with you? Get over here, pronto. I don't have coffee and I'm an inch away from dead."

"So I'll call the engraver for your tombstone."

"Ha, ha. Funny man. It's too early for funny."

"It's ten-thirty."

"Way too early for funny."

Jack moved the receiver to his other ear and closed the paper again. Despite what Mallory thought, he did have things he needed to be doing. He'd already spent more than enough time screwing around trying to read the newspaper. But in order to see to the other items on his agenda he had to be reasonably sure he could function properly without thoughts of Mallory intruding on his thoughts every five minutes.

"Jack?"

"Hmm."

"Oh. For a minute there I thought you'd hung up."

"Nope."

"But you're filling the travel cup and getting your car keys now, right?"

"Nope."

"But Layla needs us."

He lifted his brows. "How, exactly, does Layla need us?"

"She needs immediate TLC. She's waiting at Reilly's as we speak."

Jack rubbed his hand over his forehead and eyes and absently thought that he needed a shave.

"It's going to look suspicious if we don't show."

"Take the subway."

A heartbeat of a pause. "And you?"

"I'll go on my own."

"Then that'll look doubly suspicious because you always drive me."

He thought of the wreck that sat parked at the curb outside her apartment. "So get your car fixed."

"You know I can't."

What sucked was that he did know.

Jack picked up his coffee cup only to find he'd already drained the contents, then looked down at Boomer who'd lifted his head and seemed to be following Jack's end of the conversation.

"Give me ten."

Mallory hung up instantly.

THE NEXT HOUR SEEMED like a lifetime to Mallory, despite the endless supply of lifesaving, strong, hot coffee (the one cup she managed to brew at home had looked like a grease slick was floating on top) and sticky buns. Jack hadn't spoken to her during the drive over—which was really bad because it meant he was serious about his ultimatum and she didn't have any idea what to do about that. Layla looked like she'd spent the whole of last night crying and her face was a splotchy mess. And Reilly wasn't faring much better with her unsmiling expressions and long silences.

Mallory sat up, hating to admit that three sticky buns was at least a half a sticky bun too many. At least the way Reilly made them, which was really big and really sticky.

Then again, it might be the whole relationship thing. She'd spent her entire life watching her mother go from husband to boyfriend to husband again, unable to spend five solitary moments alone. Mallory had always told herself she would never do that. Would never put herself into a position where she was emotionally and financially dependent on a man, or anyone else for that matter.

She shrugged her shoulders. "I don't know what you two are so down about. I mean, the way I see it you just dodged the ultimate bullet, Layla." Her friend cringed. She switched her attention to Reilly. "And, well, you pretty much know I've had my doubts about Ben all along, Rei."

Another cringe.

She looked at Jack who was glaring at her.

"What?" she barked. "What is it about the three of you this morning? I swear, you're enough to make a corpse be sorry for dying."

Layla sighed heavily for what seemed like the umpteenth time. "You don't understand, Mallory."

"What's there to understand? I may not be Mensa material, but I've been known to rub two thoughts together."

"You don't get it," Reilly said, gesturing with her hands. "Because you're…single."

Mallory's spine snapped upright.

Jack pushed from the table. "I'm going to get some more napkins."

Coward, Mallory wanted to say.

Instead she sniffed and said, "I'm not single, I'm busy."

Layla and Reilly looked at her pitifully.

"At least I'm not crying into my coffee like you two," she said quietly. "God, you guys know how I hate whining. And right now you two are walking, talking poster children for whiners the world over."

Reilly snapped to. "For someone who claims to be a liberal, you're awfully opinionated and judgmental."

Layla agreed. "Is there a single person, group or entity that you haven't insulted at one point or another?"

Mallory honestly didn't know what to say.

Layla pushed from the table. "God, you can be so damn cynical."

"Bitter," Reilly said. "She's bitter."

Jack picked that moment to return to the table. "I'd go with cynical. To be bitter you have to have something to be bitter about. And Mallory's too scared to live."

All three women stared at him, shocked.

Making Mallory want to die.

She glanced at her two female friends, wondering what Jack had revealed with his little piece of personal insight. Was what he'd said something a friend would offer up? Of course, it probably was, but when coupled with the fact that he, as a rule, disappeared whenever one of these discussions surfaced, and never contributed anything, his change in protocol was sure to raise some brows.

Interestingly enough, however, neither Layla nor Reilly seemed to catch on.

Reilly pointed at him. "You know something? You're right."

Mallory made a face and gathered her backpack. It was chock full of everything a working producer needed.

Now, if only she could find some work.

Actually, not so much work, but capital to work with. Her current subject, The Red Gardenia, was waiting.

The Red Gardenia who haunted her at times

when she'd be better off thinking about something else. But there was just something about the subject, about Jenny Fuller, that intrigued her. The similarities in their ambitions, maybe. Whatever it was, this documentary, more than the others, was one she was driven to make.

"Jack, I think it's time for us to go," she said.

He leisurely drank his coffee. "Go where? I'm not going anywhere."

Mallory glared at him, resisting the urge to point out that Layla was watching the interplay with great curiosity. "Yes, we are. You promised to take me to that site for The Red Gardenia, remember?"

He slowly shook his head. "Nope. I don't recall."

Reilly narrowed her eyes. "Have you two had a fight or something?"

"No," Mallory said.

"Yes," Jack said at the same time.

Layla looked back and forth. "Well, which is it?"

"It doesn't matter," Mallory said quickly. "We've already kissed and made up. Haven't we, Jack?"

He didn't answer her.

Reilly made an uh-oh sound. "Doesn't look that way to me. What are you two arguing about?"

Oh, was it ever time to get out of there. Mallory grabbed Jack's arm and virtually jerked him from his chair. "We'd really like to discuss it with you, but from the looks of things you both have enough on your plates already. Don't they, Jack?"

He looked like he might like to strangle her.

The Red Gardenia had been strangled. Which Mallory really wanted to look into more—if Jack would just cooperate.

"It might help us forget our own problems," Reilly said.

"Don't worry. It's nothing the two of us can't work out," Mallory said. "Come on or we'll be late." She flashed a smile at her friends. "I'll call you both later, okay?"

They both smiled at her like they expected those phone calls to fill them in on what they were missing.

Ha! Fat chance.

WHAT WAS IT ABOUT THE woman that got under his skin so?

Jack sat behind the wheel of his '69 Chevy Camaro Z-28 and watched Mallory walk up and down Sunset Boulevard in West Hollywood, stopping every now and again to take notes. Today she wore a tight pair of faded jeans and a powder-blue T-shirt that read "Outta My Way or You're Roadkill."

Jack leaned his elbow in his open window and sighed. He only wished he didn't feel like roadkill.

He really couldn't say what had made him drive her to where she wanted to go. One minute he'd been about to spill all to Reilly and Layla, the next Mallory was giving him directions and he was following them.

He absently rubbed the back of his neck, watching as she approached someone and struck up a conversation, her pen waving in the air as she gestured with her hand. She was good at what she did. He knew that. Her documentaries were edgy and current and offered an unflinching viewpoint that not many filmmakers could capture. The word "real" sprung to mind. Her vision was real. Just like Mallory, herself, was real. Earthy. No nonsense. Sexy as hell.

And an unqualified pain in the ass.

He glanced at his wrist only to find he wasn't wearing his watch. Which wasn't surprising, because he usually didn't wear his watch. That he was even looking to see what time it was said a lot.

Didn't she understand that he had places to go, people to see?

No, he realized, she didn't. Because, unlike her, he didn't lay out his agenda like an open book.

He laid on the horn. Mallory shielded her eyes and looked in his direction while still talking to the woman she'd just introduced herself to. Then she gave him a little wave and returned her attention to her new friend.

Jack was half-tempted to drive away. But he knew he wouldn't. No matter how maddening it was to watch her curvy little bottom in those tight jeans. Or wonder at the way the light December California breeze toyed with her dark curls. Or stare at the way her mouth moved when she talked.

He forced his attention away and stared instead at the street ahead. Shit. He was in deep, wasn't he? When he'd thrown out the ultimatum last night, it had begun as a joke of sorts. But once it was out of his mouth, he'd discovered that he'd said exactly what he'd wanted to say.

And was now finding out that not only was he in deep, he was in it up to his elbows.

Not good.

Not good at all.

Especially since he had the sinking sensation that Mallory might never come to her senses and would spend the rest of her life—and his—making him live in a state of limbo.

He searched in the glove compartment for the pack of cigarettes he always kept there. Only he didn't find them. He pulled down both sun visors, glad when the driver's side one yielded a crumpled pack with one cigarette inside. He shook it out and lighted it with the car lighter.

Shit.

He filled his lungs with the acrid smoke then slowly blew it out.

Shit, shit, shit.

4

HAD JACK REALLY JUST beeped the horn at her?

Mallory gaped at the old Chevy and at Jack himself. The late morning sunlight caught his dark hair just the right way, bringing out sandy highlights that only lent to his lean, handsome appeal. She swallowed past the sudden tightness in her throat, gave him an irritated wave, then returned her attention to the prostitute she'd just introduced herself to.

Coco Cabana (she'd fought not to snicker) was more than just your average, run-of-the-mill hooker. First off, she had to be pushing fifty, a fact no amount of makeup, exercise or designer clothing could hide.

Second, she wasn't a woman at all, but a man.

Of course, Coco hadn't come right out and shared the information. And Mallory guessed that, after sundown, shadows obscured age and gender and Coco would probably be drop-dead gorgeous. But Mallory knew the score the instant she began talking to him.

He...she...whatever...was also the first person among the dozens Mallory had interviewed who knew more about The Red Gardenia than just passing rumor.

Coco lifted a cigarette to her mouth, her nails long, talonlike and blood-red. "Sure, I knew The Red Gardenia." She rolled her eyes, blue ones enhanced with spidery false eyelashes and blue eye makeup. "We both arrived in L.A. at about the same time."

Mallory's heart skipped a beat. But she still didn't completely trust the extent of Coco's knowledge. "And her real name was..."

"Jenny Fuller, of course."

Check.

"And she was from?"

Coco waved her cigarette. "Omaha, I think. Yeah. It was Nebraska."

Double check.

"Horrible tragedy, that one," Coco added with a sigh. "She had a future. Could have been a real contender."

Now that was a different take. Most people Mallory spoke to said that Jenny Fuller had probably gotten what she deserved. That Hollywood had a way of glossing over the details and that a good girl usually wasn't all she appeared.

Mallory sometimes wondered how much bad a girl from Nebraska could get into in six months.

Jenny Fuller's story wasn't all that unusual. People who came to L.A. armed only with their dreams were a dime a dozen. But the aspiring actress—whose claim to fame had been a beer ad that featured her wearing a twenties getup and a red gardenia in her hair—and her unsolved murder twenty-five years ago had come to represent all those forgotten someones whose dreams of stardom had ended, and would end, in tragedy.

Mallory looked back to Coco. She'd been digging for more info of the sympathetic and specific variety for months now. And while it seemed her personal life was in the dumps, her professional life appeared to have just taken a full tilt toward the better.

At least she hoped so.

"Look," Coco said. "If you're not going to feed me, pay me, or provide some other kind of amusement, sweetie, then I'm going to have to move on. This is a working day, you know."

Mallory tried to hide her smile. "Tell me about it."

Coco reached into her sequined purse, watched as a Cadillac with tinted windows rolled by, then reapplied peach-colored lip gloss that Mallory suspected she could see her reflection in if she leaned in close enough. "My landlord just kicked me out this morning so I need some quick cash to look for a place."

Mallory pointed her finger at the hooker then back at herself. "You and me both."

Coco leaned back in order to get a better overall

look at Mallory. "Girl, you've got to work on your appearance if you hope to get any business."

Mallory nearly choked. "Strangely enough, talking to you now is working for me." She flipped her notepad closed and considered the other, um, woman. All she had to do was say the word and Candy Cane would snap up Coco without batting an eyelash. Lost causes seemed to be her middle name. As long as Coco didn't have any animal allergies, these two people who shared the same vocation would get along famously. "Look, I have a friend in my apartment complex who would be willing to put you up until you find a place. What would it mean to you if I gave this friend a call and checked it out for you?"

"Monetarily?" Coco asked.

"Information wise."

Coco stared at her unblinkingly. "On The Red Gardenia?"

Mallory nodded.

Coco took three quick drags off her cigarette then picked a piece of tobacco off her tongue as she considered the proposition. "Where's this place?"

Mallory had her and she knew it.

Yes! Her first real lead in The Red Gardenia case.

Her smile slipped.

Well, it wasn't really a lead. But it was information that the police didn't appear to have. Of course, she had to remind herself, her goal wasn't to actually solve the case, but rather to create a more vivid picture of the young actress who had been murdered twenty-five years ago.

But if she did happen to solve the case...

She shivered all over.

Behind her Jack's horn blew again.

"Do you have time to go see the place now?" Mallory asked.

WHERE DOES SHE FIND these people?

Jack pulled up outside Mallory's apartment complex then glanced in his rearview mirror where "Coco" was staring into a round compact repairing his mask. Jack squeezed and released the steering wheel several times. Two large, faded tapestry suitcases were in his trunk. Lord only knew what they held.

Surely Mallory wasn't going to let Coco move in with her.

"Do you want to come to Candy's with me, or wait here?"

Jack knew a moment of relief. Good. She was taking the aging transvestite to Candy's. He tried to make out if Coco's cleavage was real. Well, not real, but surgically or hormonally enhanced. Oh, yeah, there were real swells there, all right. Then what would that make him? A transsexual? He supposed it all depended on if his original equipment was still intact.

He glanced at Mallory to find her glaring at him. *What?* he asked silently.

Then he realized she was piqued because he'd been staring at Coco's cleavage.

"So?" she asked.

"So what?"

"Are you going to wait here or come with us?"

He considered her for a long moment. He'd been with her for the past two hours and she had yet to breathe one word about last night. In fact, he would have thought she'd forgotten about it altogether if not for the wary shadow he saw in her brown eyes. She'd never been wary around him before.

"None of the above," he replied.

"Meaning?"

"Meaning I'm going home."

"You can't."

Jack turned to look Coco full in the face. "Do you mind waiting outside?"

"Outside? As in outside the car?"

"Is there any other outside?" he asked.

Mallory gaped at him. "I'm sorry, Coco. Domestic issues."

Mallory climbed from the car to let the aging, questionable prostitute out of the two-door car, then she got back in. He watched Coco walk to stand behind the car, out of earshot.

"You can tell her…him he can take care of his own suitcases from here on out, too."

Mallory made a sound of indignation. "What's gotten into you, Jack? You're being so...rude."

Well, well, well. Look who was calling the kettle black. "Yeah, well, that's what happens to a man when the woman he's...interested in ignores his advances for something more."

"Are we back to that again?" she asked.

"We never left it, Mall."

She got out of the car again, then popped her dark head of curls back through the open window. "Stay put. You and I...we need to powwow."

Powwow? Had she really just said powwow?

But as he sat watching her struggle with Coco's suitcases, then waddle toward Candy's, her jeans molded to her pert little bottom, he knew he wasn't going anywhere.

Damn it.

He picked up his travel coffee cup and put it to his lips only to find it empty.

He grimaced. Was he seeing a pattern here or what?

What remained was whether or not he had the balls to do anything about it.

LATER THAT NIGHT Mallory flopped down on what she thought might be her couch hiding under clean laundry she had draped over it the day before. Of course, the dryer would have to break down in the middle of her load. And she hadn't had a chance to fold the things and put them away yet. She supposed she might do it now, but...well, as she looked at Jack, other, more important, things came to mind.

Jack stood in the middle of the room, staring down at her while wearing the same expression he'd been wearing all day. At least five times she'd had to talk him out of leaving her to go home. And each time he'd grown sulkier and sulkier.

"Are we done now?" he muttered, his hands fisted and shoved deep into the pockets of his cargo jeans.

Mallory allowed her gaze to drift over him. He was quite a man, this Jack Daniels. Wherever they went, women openly ogled him, making no secret of their interest. Not that Jack paid any attention. He was completely oblivious to the attention he received. And when he did catch wind of it—like when she, Layla and Reilly jokingly threw cat calls his way every now and again—he'd mumble and curse and move out of sight as fast as he could.

Now she watched him shift his weight from his right foot to his left, his present discomfort level rising with the sweep of her gaze from his loafer-clad feet to his snug black T-shirt.

She'd begun the exercise of giving him a provocative once-over to tease him. And while it was working—as she'd known it would—she also found herself getting a little more than turned on.

Mmm...

"Can I leave now?" he said, obviously clenching his teeth.

"Nope," she said, using the word he'd used on her all day.

His bedroom-brown eyes narrowed. "Mallory..."

"Jack..." she said, reaching for the hem of her T-shirt and pulling it over her head.

She knew he loved to see her undergarments. She might not be a total fashion plate, but just as she took extra care in picking her comment-laden T-shirts, she also took great pleasure in choosing her lingerie carefully. The bra she had on today was deep purple with demi cups and sexy lace edging. She sat up and gave a little shimmy as if trying to get more comfortable, satisfied when his gaze dropped to her cleavage and his pupils instantly took over the color of his irises.

Yeah, baby. Show Mama how much you want her.

Her nipples hardened under his steady scrutiny and she pushed her breasts out even further. They strained against the demi cups and she knew that Jack was wishing they'd just pop right out.

"Mallory..." he said again in warning, though most of the conviction had drained away.

She popped the front button on her jeans, allowing the zipper to slide partway down on its own steam to reveal her matching pair of purple lace panties.

She watched Jack swallow hard.

Mallory tried to formulate her next move, but the truth was her brain was starting to feel a bit muddled and the heat gathering between her thighs was downright distracting. His gaze moved back to her face as if he was searching for some way to combat his growing physical need. So she licked her lips, making sure to do it slowly and provocatively.

"Now," she said, surprised to find her voice so husky. She'd been going after the effect but even she couldn't have predicted the outcome. Candy, with her throaty cadence, had nothing on her. "I think we'd better discuss this, um, whole no-sex issue."

She thought she heard a choking sound, but she couldn't be sure. But she did know that Jack was looking a little rough around the edges. He nodded. "Yes. I think we should, too."

She scooted over on the couch, pushed a few items of clothing out of the way, then patted the cushion. "Why don't you sit down next to me?"

He did nothing for long, silent moments, then he shook his head. "I, um, don't think that's such a great idea."

Mallory smiled. "Why?"

"Because we won't discuss the sex issue. We'll be having sex."

"Exactly what I had in mind."

"Exactly why I'm staying right where I am."

She saw his face take on a competitive appearance. Damn. Maybe she *could* use a pointer or two from Candy.

"Okay," she said slowly. "Then I'll come to you."

Jack seemed so surprised by the proposal that he didn't move when she pushed off the couch then stood before him, not touching, but definitely close enough to.

Of course, if she had a hope of getting this femme fatale role down pat, she'd have to learn to quiet her own riot of emotions whenever she came this close to Jack.

"I'm not going to kiss you," Jack said, though his voice was hoarse.

"Mmm. You don't have to." She looked at the solid column of his throat. "But you don't mind if I kiss you, do you?"

He opened his mouth to answer her but she put her palm over his mouth, trapping his words there. Then she tilted her head to press her lips against the front of his throat, then the side, breathing in the fresh scent of his skin, absorbing the warmth radiating from him like a fine musk. He swallowed again and she smiled, blinking her eyes so that her lashes dragged across his skin.

"Come on, Jack," she murmured, itching to feel

his hands on her. All over her. She wanted him to explore every inch of her flesh in that possessive way of his, lay claim to her. But he didn't budge an inch.

"We are not having sex, Mall."

She smiled and slowly began kissing her way down to the collar of his T-shirt. She tugged the soft cotton out of his jeans then worked her fingertips under the hem, not stopping until she felt the hard muscles of his abdomen. How he kept in such great shape, she didn't know. A more inactive man, she'd never met. But whatever he was doing was working. He was a fine, chiseled specimen of male virility. And just looking at him made her want to rip off her clothes and beg for him to sex her.

She tugged down the collar of his T-shirt and ran her tongue the length of his collarbone. Of course, right now it looked like she was going to have to be the one doing the sexing.

Which was all right with her....

Under his T-shirt, she ran her fingertips down his sides, and he shivered. She smiled then started to slide down the length of him. When he would have protested, she chased the air from his lungs by suctioning her lips to his stomach, then sticking her tongue into his navel, which was a delicious innie. When she was finally kneeling in front of him, she easily found the thick ridge straining against the front of his cargo pants, all the while keeping her gaze plastered to his. It didn't do much to her ego to see his quiet wariness. But there was no denying he was turned on so she pushed ahead.

The sound of his zipper opening filled the room, then within seconds his long, thick length filled her palms.

She often heard some women complain about having to perform oral. But Mallory had always loved exploring every millimeter of a man's turgid flesh. Enjoyed feeling the knob of a man's arousal in her mouth, the shallow dip as her tongue moved over and down the shaft. She liked applying suction and watching a grown man nearly cry at her expert attentions.

She loved everything about it. Especially when it came to Jack. In the beginning, she could tell that he hadn't had many blowjobs before. The first time he'd nearly ejaculated when she'd simply breathed on him. Now he was able to exercise a bit more control.

Mallory closed her eyes and took a deep breath, reveling in the scent of his desire. She gently squeezed his hair-covered sac, finding the orbs below hard and swollen. Then she fit her mouth over the tip of his erection, not quite covering the head, following the small, narrow opening with the tip of her tongue then sucking.

Jack's hips automatically bucked forward, as if

trying to force a fuller meeting. Mallory pulled back and smiled.

"Big Jack may be saying no, but little Jack looks like he's all for a little slap and tickle," she murmured, running her fingers down his shaft then back up again.

"Watch who you're calling little," he said.

She grasped the base of his arousal almost tightly then fit him inside her mouth so that the tip pressed against the inside of her cheek. She swirled her tongue as far around his girth as it would go— which wasn't far—then moved him to the other side of her mouth and did the same there, licking and smoothing, then finally sucking.

Jack's tortured groan filled her ears and made heat explode through her own groin. She'd found there were few things that turned her on more than turning Jack on.

She took her mouth off him, then positioned herself straight on, making a shallow channel with her tongue then sliding her mouth over him as far as she could before the natural choking instinct kicked in. The length she couldn't fit inside she grasped with the fingers of her right hand while her left cupped the sac below.

Oh, yes. She could taste the bittersweet evidence of his seed coat her tongue as she closed her lips around his width then moved her mouth forward and back with smooth, easy strokes. On each pass she increased the suction and swirled her tongue around and over, mimicking the movement with her hand along the lower part of his shaft.

He was ready. She could feel it. Could tell in the rapid, irregular rhythm of his breathing. The way his hands had finally moved from his sides to grasp her head, not quite guiding her but not stopping her, either, his fingers tangling in the curly strands. Mallory squeezed her own thighs together and shuddered, finding herself near climax. Astonishing what this guy did to her even when he was doing nothing.

She increased the rhythm of her mouth and her hand. Then she squeezed his sac and his shaft and suddenly halted the movement of her mouth, sucking hard.

His hips bucked forward and he exploded in her mouth like a shot of streaming water. Except his semen was thick and hot and she had to swallow several times to prevent it from running down the side of her chin.

Finally the stream stopped and Mallory sat back on her heels, leisurely lapping him clean with her tongue as she massaged his balls. She pressed one final kiss to the tip of his still-hard penis then glanced up at him, triumphant.

"Care to take back yesterday's ultimatum?" she whispered huskily, all too ready to move the action to her bedroom.

Jack's eyes narrowed while he clearly fought to even out his breathing.

Then he did something that shocked her straight

to her toes. He reached down, tucked his arousal back into his pants, then zipped them up. "Nope," he said.

Mallory couldn't form the words to respond to him.

He ran his hand under her chin, gave it a squeeze and said, "Thanks."

Mallory made a sound of indignation as she sat flat on her bottom. "We have sex and that's all you can say?"

He shrugged as he tucked his T-shirt back into his jeans. "We didn't have sex, Mallory. You forced me to accept a blowjob. There's a difference."

"What?" It took her several attempts to get to her feet because her mind wasn't concentrated on the action. "You've got to be kidding me? It's called 'oral sex,' Jack. The emphasis on sex. And whether you want to admit it or not, we just had it."

"Mmm. Maybe. But my ultimatum still stands."

Mallory felt something toward Jack that she had never felt before. Anger. No, no, not anger. That was too tame a word. She felt…enraged.

"Good night, Mall," he said, then gave her a kiss on the forehead.

Mallory watched him walk through the door and close it after himself, incapable of doing anything but standing and gaping after him.

5

THE FOLLOWING MORNING—a quarter after twelve, actually, but to Mallory it was morning—Mallory sat across from Coco in Candy's chintzy dining room drinking the vanilla blend instant stuff that Candy called coffee while Mallory assessed Coco. Just inside the kitchen Candy pretended to be busy, but Mall knew she was listening to every word they were saying.

"You look like hell," Coco told Mallory, her nails perfectly manicured, her hair teased within an inch of its life, her makeup artfully applied, her white silk robe without a wrinkle as she drank from a rose-covered porcelain teacup.

Mallory grimaced at her own cup, not even sure how to lift the sucker. The grip looked far too small and delicate. She settled on grabbing it like a glass and nearly downing the contents. "It's called my morning look. Can you tell mornings and I don't get along really well?"

This morning she chose an older T-shirt she hadn't worn in a while. It read I Hate People.

Unfortunately she was also broke, which meant

no money to buy coffee—or filters for that matter—so she'd been forced into the world of people—more specifically Candy—to seek out a jolt of much-needed caffeine. She stared at her cup. Did this instant stuff even have caffeine?

Of course it didn't help that she hadn't gotten much sleep, either. When Jack had walked out on her last night, she'd stood in the same spot staring after him for a full half hour before she'd finally flopped back to the couch. She'd stared at the ceiling for another good hour before a coherent thought had entered her stunned brain.

He'd just walked out. Just like that. And had treated her no better than…

What? A one-nighter?

She made a face. No. To be a true one-nighter, she would have gotten as well as given.

Well, in her definition anyway.

But Jack had just walked out and left her hanging. And left her revisiting that decade-old debate about what acts actually constituted sex. Was oral sex, sex? Or was it a form of petting? Jack made her come once merely by licking her breasts. So had that been sex? Of course not.

Which left the question of whether a blowjob was sex.

She picked up her cup again only to find she'd already drained it. What was she thinking about, anyway? It didn't really matter whether oral sex was sex. Not at this point. What did was that Jack seemed determined to go full steam ahead with his intention not to have sex with her unless she agreed to broaden the parameters of her idea of their relationship and tell Layla and Reilly about it.

Which was funny, because without the sex there wasn't much of a relationship, anyway, was there?

She blinked, almost surprised to find Coco sitting across from her. It had taken Candy's banging of a pan to bring her back to the here and now. And it would do her good to keep in mind that she needed to advance her career plans today or her plan to succeed in L.A. would fail. Completely and miserably.

She squinted at Coco. She looked well turned out in the diffused light. In fact, she looked presentable enough to be filmed.

"Can you hold a minute?" she asked, holding up a finger.

She pushed from the table and chased Candy out of the kitchen while she dialed her cameraman's home phone number on her cell. Harris picked up on the third ring.

She outlined the situation for him then said, "I need you here in fifteen."

Silence.

"Harris? Are you still there?"

"Yeah, I'm still here. I'm just waiting for the part where you tell me you have my money."

Mallory nearly choked. "Get this segment for me and I guarantee I'll have your money by day's end."

"That's what you said last month. Then three weeks ago. Two weeks ago. Last—"

"All right, all right, I get the picture," she grumbled. She paced back and forth across Candy's neat kitchen. How come her kitchen didn't look this way? Well, gee, maybe if she cleaned it, it would. "I know this is difficult, Harris. But you know I haven't been paid yet, either."

"And that concerns me how?"

She raised her brows. "That concerns you because if I get paid, you get paid."

She opened Candy's refrigerator. Skim milk, fruits, a variety of cheeses, a half-full bottle of white wine, butter, yogurt and—bingo—a Sara Lee cherry cheesecake container. She took it out. Candy must have just taken it out of the freezer and put it into the refrigerator to thaw because it was still frozen. Not that it mattered. Mallory found a fork and made an inroad, dropping a frozen cherry on her T-shirt as she ate.

Sugar was a great, if temporary, replacement for caffeine.

"Look, Mall, I've already lined up another gig," Harris said. "Something that actually pays. Imagine that."

"You'll get paid by me!" She stared at where

the cherry seemed to fill the "a" in "hate" on her T-shirt. She peeled the cherry from the cotton, eyed it, then stuck it into her mouth.

"I need to get paid in this millennium, Mall. Sorry. I can't help you."

She made a sound of frustration.

"Oh. And you still owe me the money, by the way."

He hung up.

Mallory stared at the silent cell phone. What was it with her and men lately? It seemed that every time she turned around one was screwing her.

Wrong choice of words. Because if she was being screwed—by Jack more specifically—then maybe she wouldn't be in such a foul mood this morning. Afternoon. Whatever.

"Hey! That's tonight's dessert," Candy said, sweeping into the kitchen and fighting her for the cheesecake.

"You might as well let me have it," Mall said. "I got my germs all over it already."

"Germs, I can handle. If I couldn't then, boy, would I ever be in the wrong line of business," the pretty prostitute said.

Mallory rolled her eyes. Her good luck meter had just bottomed out to zero.

Then again, she didn't think it had rarely ever read higher than that since coming to L.A. five years ago. She could count the three times she'd lucked out on three fingers on one hand. First there was landing her virgin producing gig (a children's show on child abuse). Second was meeting Layla, Reilly and Jack. And third was sleeping with Jack.

"Get your own Sara Lee," Candy said.

Mallory sighed heavily then went back into the other room where Coco still sat at the dining room table. When you looked at her...him...in profile, he was every bit the alluring female, if a bit of an aging alluring female.

"Candy?" she asked tentatively, wondering how many points she'd lost with the Sara Lee bit. "Do you still have that camcorder?"

JACK SAT AT HIS COMPUTER, Boomer lay in the corner of the room on his mammoth red pillow and the cursor on the flat-screen monitor blinked at Jack relentlessly, pointing out the utter blackness of the screen.

He leaned back in his chair and looked out into the kitchen at the telephone extension there. It was two in the afternoon and Mallory had yet to call.

He stared at the screen again, fingers poised above the keyboard. Of course, Mallory could still very well be sleeping. Or she may have forgotten to charge her cell, which was her only telephone because her land line had been disconnected a week or so ago.

He glanced down at his notes, which were little

more than thought fragments that usually sparked enough material for ten columns.

Now he couldn't seem to generate enough to write a solitary sentence, much less come up with a topic for the piece.

The issue would come out in January. Another new year…winter in California…New Year's resolutions…La Niña, El Niño…roadwork on Route 101…Christmas gifts that needed taking back…

Nothing. Not one single idea jumped out at him.

Modern-day women who thought romance was a thing of the past…

He stretched his neck and closed his eyes. Oh, he was so not going to go there. For one thing, he was much too close to the subject. For another, he'd probably piss Mallory off enough that she wouldn't be interested in being his friend anymore, much less his lover.

He remembered the incredible oral sex she'd given him last night and leaned back and grinned. The woman ought to give classes, he thought. Oh, sure, he'd had his share of blowjobs before, but it had seemed he'd always had to force the issue. And when he'd gotten them, the women had always seemed to be just this side of hanging their heads over the toilet. Watching a woman go down on you wasn't much fun when her face was green and she looked like she might barf at any minute.

But Mallory…

He stretched his hands behind his neck. Mallory genuinely looked like she enjoyed giving him pleasure. Interestingly enough, she seemed to get as much pleasure out of the act as he did. Which didn't make much sense to him, but, hey, he wasn't going to argue the point. He just loved watching that saucy mouth of hers sink down over his hard-on, and her tongue flip up and around, the mere sight nearly bringing him to orgasm. And forget the naughty look on her face.

He glanced at the photo on the corner of his desktop. It was a shot of him, Mallory, Layla and Reilly taken at the beach last summer. They were all sunburned and happy, smiling goofily into the camera lens. It had been before Layla had met Sam and Reilly, Ben.

He stared back at the blinking cursor. Hmm…perhaps if he geared the piece more toward the problems Layla and Reilly were having with modern-day relationships…

Yeah, and risk destroying the entire circle of friends, period.

No thanks. Sometimes he was convinced that Layla, Reilly and Mallory were the only things keeping him from diving head first into the sealed bottle of Russian vodka he kept sitting on the sideboard gathering dust.

He looked at the bottle now and felt only the slightest tinge of desire to crack it open.

Three years ago he'd felt a ravenous craving.

Two years, he'd salivated after it.

Last year he'd actually held it in his hands, coming this close to breaking the seal to see if he could handle just one shot.

And now he wanted to throw the damn thing right out the window.

Hmm…had he ever done a piece on fellatio?

Oh, yeah. He could see *L.A. Monthly* senior editor's reaction to that one. Patrick Kenway looked like he hadn't had a good blowjob in twenty years. If he'd ever had a good one without paying for it.

The phone rang.

Boomer lifted his head and gave a hopeful whine.

Jack pushed from the chair and ambled into the kitchen to pick up the cordless receiver.

"Daniels, here," he said, wondering if Mallory had just woken up and was in dire need of coffee.

A long-suffering sigh then a familiar voice said, "Must you answer the phone in that manner, Jackson?"

His mother.

He instantly wished he hadn't answered at all. "Had I known it was you calling, I would have considered an alternate greeting."

"They do have that caller ID now, you know," she told him. "Great little device that."

He glanced at his telephone, which supported the technology, but he didn't subscribe to it. Anyway, even if he did, his parents called so seldom he probably wouldn't even have bothered to program them. Not to mention that Lord only knew where they would be calling from.

"How are you, Jackson?"

"Fine. You?"

"Very well, thank you."

"And Dad?"

"Your father's well, thanks for asking."

Jack felt cold. Having these stilted conversations with his mother had always chilled him to the point that he'd want to break out one of the few sweaters he owned. There was something so…stiff about the whole exchange. Unnatural. It's not that he didn't care about how his parents were, but he got the impression that if they weren't doing well, they wouldn't tell him. And that he'd be breaking some sort of unwritten code if he told them that his life sucked big, fat cucumbers right now.

That made him recall Mallory's expert attentions last night and cleared his throat. Definitely not something he wanted to think about while talking to his mother.

"Your father and I returned to town late last night and I thought you and I could have lunch," Celia Daniels was saying. "Is tomorrow all right with you?"

"Do you always give everyone such short notice?"

She laughed delicately. "Jackson, everyone else is usually doing something. But not you."

He grimaced, all these mentions lately of his lack of ambition beginning to bug him big time.

"One o'clock tomorrow at Le Dome," she suggested.

"Noon at Benardo's Hideaway."

A sigh, then, "Okay, if you insist. Oh, and why don't you bring that girl you've been seeing?"

Jack absently scratched his head. The girl he'd been seeing? There was no possible way his parents could know he was seeing anyone. Especially since Mallory insisted in keeping their extracurricular activities under cover.

Then he remembered the Sunday three months ago when Mallory had opened his front door to find his parents making one of their very rare surprise visits.

"I'm not seeing anyone," he said.

"Oh. Very well then. Come alone."

"Will Dad be there?"

"Your father will be otherwise occupied."

Which could mean anything ranging between he had a golf engagement to he had an appointment for a rectal exam.

"Fine. I'll see you tomorrow then."

He hung up the phone and stood there for a long minute trying not to grind his teeth.

Talking to his mother always had that impact on him.

For a guy who pretty much had his shit together—at least right now anyway—just hearing the sound of his mother's voice was enough to make him feel sick. Oh, his parents had always provided well for him. He'd always had the best nannies, attended the top schools, worn all the best clothes, eaten all the best foods. Funny, but he recalled that his parents liked to use the word "best" a lot. But being an eight-year-old boy sitting in the Italian marble-tiled kitchen with nothing but a nanny as his companion, eating blackened salmon and steamed artichoke hearts for dinner and dying to tell someone how he got his black eye... Well, it wasn't all it was cracked up to be. It had always seemed his parents were away somewhere important.

"Mummy and Da are at a very important charity event/meeting/dinner/ball," his Irish nanny, Maeve, used to tell him when he'd asked. The word "important" had also been an overused word in the Daniels house. Important and best.

Of course it wasn't long before he'd stopped asking.

Sure, his parents had attended all the important milestones. High school graduation. College graduation. His track finals. But they'd seemed more interested in touting his accomplishments to fellow braggart parents than in spending any real time watching him. He'd broken the school record once in the long jump, and his father had been standing not twenty feet away, but neither of his parents had seen it. His mother had been too busy seeing to her makeup in her compact and his father had been chortling with another father next to him.

Scheduled play dates with the "right" friends, sports, the debate club—as he got older it seemed his own life started filling up with only the "best" things, "important" events. But none of it made up for what was lacking in his life. Of course, he hadn't known what was lacking because in order to know he would have had to have some experience in the area. Since he hadn't, it had been all too easy to fall into his first vodka bottle when he was thirteen and egged on by friends. And he hadn't climbed back out until he was twenty.

He crossed back to his computer in the other room. What did it mean when a guy didn't like his own parents?

"Oh, get over yourself," he muttered aloud. Those were the words of his AA sponsor, Will Harding, ten years ago. *"So you're a poor little rich boy. So what? The instant you turned eighteen and became an adult the reins of control were passed on to you. You and only you are responsible for your actions now, buddy. Get used to it. And, damn it, start doing something meaningful with them."*

The simple words had made so much sense to

him that it was almost as if a hypnotist had snapped his fingers next to his ear and woken him from a long trance.

And a new word had been introduced into his vocabulary. "Meaningful."

Since then he'd done a lot of mulling over the meaning of the word. It was as hefty as "best" and "important," but different.

Meaningful...

He blinked, finding he'd typed the word across his computer screen.

Jack leaned back.

Yeah, there you go. Perhaps he could explore the many aspects of the word "meaningful" for his January piece.

And maybe, just maybe, it would help him find his way through the complicated maze that was his life with Mallory Woodruff.

He'd long ago accepted that his life with his parents was a lost cause.

6

MALLORY SAT IN THE middle of her living room floor, having cleared a spot so she could spread out all the information she had on The Red Gardenia case. From coroner pictures, to the original police report, to the changing detective names assigned to the unsolved case throughout the years, she'd compiled reams of information about one enigmatic Jenny Fuller.

She leafed through the copies of the photos she'd collected until she came to the one of a seventeen-year-old Jenny featured in a family portrait with her parents and four brothers and sister. According to her notes, the shot was taken a mere month before Jenny graduated from high school, packed her mom's home-baked chocolate chip cookies into her simple leather suitcase and took a Greyhound bus from Omaha to L.A. to make it in Hollywood.

Mallory squinted at the shot, trying to read the young woman's eyes. She looked…happy. Had she known then that she was going to L.A.? Could that be the reason for her expression? Or at that point was Hollywood little more than a blurry dream?

The growling of her stomach distracted her. She rubbed at it then put the picture down and looked at her watch.

Midnight.

Was it really midnight already?

And she hadn't eaten anything all day except the cheesecake she'd snuck at Candy's place.

She leaned back on her hands and stretched her neck. After purloining Candy's handheld camcorder, she'd spent the next two hours—all the time she'd had on the one video tape—talking to Coco about what she knew about The Red Gardenia.

Too bad her VCR had busted about four months ago. And since Candy had insisted Mallory leave the camera at her place (what, did she think she might hock it?), she couldn't watch a single second of the footage she'd gotten.

Of course, she did know one person who had a perfectly functioning VCR and who would be up this late....

She closed her eyes, seeing a clear picture of Jack sitting in the middle of his brown sofa, Boomer at his feet, a soda in his hand as he watched Letterman.

The odd clenching sensation was so strong she almost doubled up.

Of course, that was just as likely due to hunger pains as it was to missing Jack.

She pushed up off the floor, leaving the file contents strewn about, and ambled into the kitchen. She went through all the cupboards and the refrigerator, finding nothing but a slice of single wrapped Velveeta cheese and a few broken taco shells. She put a taco on a plate, flattened it with a smack of her hand, then put pieces of the cheese on top. Twenty seconds later she had a tea plate of sorry-looking nachos.

She walked into the next room and plopped back down in the middle of the living room, absently looking over the material.

She would not, could not call Jack.

She finished off the taco and cheese, cursing when the food emerged little more than a pathetic appetizer and made her stomach growl even louder.

She groaned, resisting the urge to lick whatever remaining cheese was stuck to the plate, then pushed it aside on the floor next to her, trying to concentrate on the case.

Essentially she had reached a dead end. While she'd thought Coco would give her more information with which to work—and she had managed to color in some of the personal information, verify it and add to it—Coco had professed to know absolutely nothing about the circumstances surrounding the murder.

No, as far as Coco knew, Jenny Fuller had never hooked.

No, she hadn't associated with any shady characters. She'd only been in town for six months and hadn't had many friends. She got up early and went back to her one-room apartment early, extra careful about talking to strangers like every other corn-fed girl from the Midwest who'd just moved to the big city.

Mallory read through her notes. Jenny had landed a bit part on a soap opera. More of a walk on, really, than a part with lines. She had just auditioned for a toothpaste commercial. And following her stint in that beer ad, she'd given her portfolio to a lower-rung but moderately respectable agency that was now big time.

The information reminded her so much of her own past five years in L.A. Pounding the pavement. Hoping for that one big break…

She shook her head to clear her mind.

Who would want to kill Jenny? And in such a cruel and brutal way?

Mallory had left the photographs from the murder scene tucked into a manila envelope. She'd seen them often enough that the images seemed etched into her corneas. A cord of some sort had been used to choke her, the action so violent that she'd had a half-inch deep wound at the front of her neck. A mafia grin they called it, although those were usually caused by a knife.

If that wasn't bad enough in and of itself, Jenny

had also been partially dismembered. None of the missing pieces had been recovered.

Mallory shuddered just thinking about it. What sicko would want somebody's feet?

The police had ruled it a sex crime, even though there had been no evidence of semen on the body or of vaginal penetration. In fact, what still puzzled everybody was that Jenny Fuller, aka The Red Gardenia, had still been a virgin in a town and at a time when few girls her age were virgins.

Mallory crossed her legs and pondered that one.

A knock sounded at the door.

She jumped. It was after midnight, and given the nature of the material she was reviewing…well, a stranger knocking at the door would creep anyone out, wouldn't it?

She got to her feet then walked over and looked through the peephole.

Jack!

JACK TRIED TO KEEP A hold on Boomer's leash, but the instant Mallory opened the door, the old hound suddenly found energy enough to fight him for control and bound into her apartment. The big lug nearly knocked her over in his quest to lick every inch of her face.

Hmm…actually the prospect didn't emerge all that unappealing, even to Jack. Mallory looked like she could use a good face licking.

He cleared his throat and held up the steaming pizza box in his other hand. "Someone ordered delivery?"

Mallory had crouched down to roughhouse with Boomer, but the instant he said the words she snapped to her feet and threw her arms around Jack. "Oh, you don't know what a lifesaver you are!"

Jack stumbled backward, knocked off track to find Mallory so close. Too close. In fact, she was close enough to kiss. Jack watched her decadent mouth as she moved her hands up his arms. If she were to kiss him right now, his ultimatum would be instant history.

Instead she snatched the pizza box from his hand and opened it as she walked toward the paper-strewn dining room table. She had her hand inside so that when she dropped the box she was miraculously holding a piece.

"Mmm...mmm...mmm...mmm." Mallory didn't usually make sounds when she ate, but now she was surprisingly loud. She stood completely still, with her eyes closed in apparent bliss, and she chewed and chewed and chewed until the piece was gone. Then she licked her fingers.

Jack shook his head. It looked like she still hadn't gotten the financial backing she needed. And since he'd known the contents of her kitchen by heart, he hadn't been able to enjoy Letterman one wit knowing she was probably starving to death.

A friend wouldn't let a friend go hungry, he'd rationalized.

He allowed his gaze to travel the length of her compact, dynamite body while she continued making appreciative sounds. Of course, a friend wouldn't be looking at another friend in the hungry way he was looking at her, either. But, damn, he'd missed her. You would have thought a month had passed instead of twenty-four hours since he'd last seen her.

Besides, he'd made up his mind not to make it easy for her to forget the ultimatum. Whenever they were together sex seemed to be foremost on both their minds. So he intended to put them together as often as he could.

His gaze traveled back up to her face to find her watching him speculatively.

He lifted the six-pack of ice-cold beer he held in his other hand along with Boomer's leash.

Mallory reached into the open box for another piece of pizza at the same time as she held his gaze. She fed Boomer a piece of pepperoni, the old hound making as much noise as she had while he ate it.

"That's not good for him, you know," Jack said.

"I know. But nothing really great is ever good for you." She patted Boomer, earning her a wild wagging of his tail. "Isn't that right, bucko?"

She stood up and waved the piece of pizza at him

before she took a bite. "Any particular reason for this?" she asked around a mouthful of food.

He should have known she wouldn't merely accept the pizza. Should have expected Mallory's ceaseless questions. Of course, he'd intended to avoid them. And he still intended to follow that route.

Jack took a beer out, popped the top, then handed it to her.

"Thanks," she said, taking a swig. "Answer my question."

Then again, maybe he'd have to do a little explaining. Jack put the rest of the six-pack down on the dining room table then crossed to sit on the couch. "Let's just say it's my way of saying I'm sorry."

She remained standing where she was but swiveled a bit to keep meeting his gaze head on. "What did you say?" she asked, squinting.

She probably hadn't heard him, what with her and Boomer chewing up a storm.

Jack rested his forearms on his jean-clad knees then clasped his hands. "I said I'm sorry."

Mallory's chewing stopped altogether although she still held a good three quarters of a piece of pizza. With her free hand, she grabbed a chair, swung it around, then straddled it to face him. "This I've got to hear. Jack Daniels, apologizing? It can't be."

"Eat your pizza."

"I'm eating, I'm eating." And she was, making quick work of devouring the second large slice. "Tell me again."

He grimaced at her. "You don't have to make a big ceremony out of it."

"Sure I do. Simply because you usually don't do anything that requires an apology." She plucked a napkin from the top of the pizza box, her eyes narrowing slightly. "So tell me, Jack...what, exactly, are you apologizing for?"

"For leaving here the way I did last night."

He stared at his hands rather than at her.

The truth was he'd been tortured ever since he'd walked out her door twenty-four hours ago. He'd been callous and cold and so outside his usual mode of operation that it had taken him a while to convince himself he'd done it.

"I see," she said, nodding. She took another long pull from the beer bottle. Jack ignored the movement, suddenly craving a bit of the alcohol himself, although beer had never been his drink of choice. She waved the bottle. "So the other thing...that still stands?"

Jack felt a grin coming on. "The no sex thing?" He mimicked her nodding. "Oh, yes. Definitely still on."

Her nodding turned to shaking. "I don't get you, Jack. I really don't." She pointed at him with the hand holding the bottle. "Sometimes I think I should be doing a documentary about you, you know, if just so I can get to know you better."

He blinked at her odd statement. "You know me better than anyone else on Earth."

"Do I? Because I don't feel like I do."

Jack thought about it for a minute. Okay, so he didn't like to do a whole lot of talking about himself. His parents and family? Brief details in any conversation. His alcohol addiction? A Cliffs Notes. How he filled his days? Nobody's business but his own.

He scratched his neck then smoothed down the back of his hair. "Tell me how you don't think you know me and I'll point out how you do."

She considered him for a time before responding. "Does that mean you'll answer any question I ask? Or that you'll avoid answering any of my questions?"

He merely grinned.

She rolled her eyes and sighed, the pizza and the beer forgotten as she crossed her arms on top of the back of the chair then rested her chin on them. "Hmm...okay, I'll bite." She gestured toward the papers littering the floor. "I've hit a stone wall here, anyway."

Jack looked around, noticing the information on The Red Gardenia laid out in Mallory's normal organized chaotic way at his feet. "Was your new friend able to shed any light on the case?"

"Coco? No. And don't try to change the subject."

Jack leaned back in the sofa and crossed his arms over his chest. "So ask your question already."

"Question? As in one? Singular?"

He nodded. "Let's start with one and see where that takes us."

"Cagey."

"Careful."

"Why?"

He raised a brow. "Is that your question?"

"Is 'why?' my question?"

"Uh-huh."

She rubbed her chin with her thumb. "Actually it is." She sat up a bit. "Why are you off-putting, quiet, evasive and reluctant to mention anything about your life?"

He lifted his other brow to join the first. "That's one question?"

She smiled. "That's a trademark Mallory Woodruff question."

"Well, then, far be it from me to avoid it then."

He dropped his arms so that they lay more on his stomach than his chest. Boomer yawned then stretched out at Mallory's feet, the little traitor. It was almost as if he were saying, "Trust me, the answer's not all that interesting."

"Well?" Mallory said.

"Give a guy a second to think of a response."

"You had a second."

He leaned forward. "Okay. First of all, I don't happen to think that I'm off-putting, quiet, evasive or...what was the other one?"

"Reluctant to mention anything about your life," she reminded him.

"Ah. Well, that one...maybe."

"Why?"

"Admitting that I am isn't enough?"

Her smile widened. "Nope."

"Pity."

He drew in a deep breath then slowly exhaled. "Maybe because there really isn't anything about my life worth sharing."

"Mmm. Maybe. Then again, maybe not." She rested her cheek against her forearm and he could tell she was getting tired. Likely from not having eaten much of anything all day and now gorging until her stomach was about to pop. "Tell me how you pass your day."

"Easy. Driving you around since your car broke down."

"When you're not driving me around."

He shrugged and realized that Boomer wasn't sleeping but rather was watching him out from under droopy eyelids. "I get up at around six—"

That got Mallory's attention. "Six? Gad, what do you do? Go fishing or something?"

He grinned. "I sometimes go for a run, sometimes I don't."

He watched her visibly shudder.

"Then, depending on what day it is, I work on my column…"

Mallory moved her hand in a circular motion. "Go on."

He cleared his throat. "On Tuesday and Thursday mornings I go to UCLA where I teach a class on journalism. And next semester I've signed up to teach one on fiction writing."

Mallory's head snapped up from her arms. "What?" She shook her head quickly as if trying to make sense of his words. "Pass that last one by me again because I don't think I quite caught it."

He shrugged and did as she asked.

"You…teach. At UCLA. A graduate course."

He nodded, noticing she ignored the bit about the fiction writing. Good thing, because he wasn't particularly willing to share that part of his life yet. "Mmm-hmm. Is that so hard to believe?"

"No…not hard to believe. Just surprising. How long have you been doing this?"

"Since last year."

"And you didn't tell me?"

He chuckled softly. "Trust me, Mall, there's

enough drama going on in your life to dominate any conversation.''

"Oh, no. Don't you blame that one on me. You've been teaching a class on—which days was it?—Tuesdays and—"

"Thursdays."

"Right, Thursday mornings, and I didn't know about it? That's a big omission."

"You're usually still sleeping then."

"Another cop-out." She rested her chin in her hands again. "Do Layla and Reilly know?"

"I don't know. I may or may not have mentioned something to Layla."

"And that would be because?"

"Because I wanted to demonstrate how one goes about asking a doctor fact-finding questions."

"Ah."

"What did that mean?"

"That meant that I'm more than a little miffed that Layla knows and I don't."

Jack pulled loosely at his collar. "I said she may or may not know. I'm not clear on how I asked the question."

"Meaning you may have posed it in a way that implied it was your own personal curiosity."

"Possibly."

Mallory sighed heavily. "I just don't get you, Jack. Here you are living this secret life none of us knows anything about—"

"I teach, Mall. You make it sound like I'm dealing drugs on street corners every night."

"You might as well be. At least in my book." Her sexy face scrunched up as she thought. "I mean, if you've kept that a secret, what else are you hiding? And, the bigger question is, why?"

God, but she was beautiful. Sometimes he felt he could just watch her for hours. He didn't have to say anything. Just watch her talk. Watch her expressions as her razor-sharp mind chip-chip-chipped away at something that interested her. He'd never really felt that way about a woman before. Never really felt that way about another person before, period.

But Mallory...

There was something unique and fresh and undiluted about the way she approached life. Someone showed up at the door, she didn't rush around trying to clean up the place. She was who she was and she made no apologies for it. He glanced around the cluttered place. Of course, he wouldn't mind if she was a little neater.

But that wasn't his point. The point was that Mallory seemed to know right where she stood in the world and was quite happy about it. Not happy about failing to get the financial backing she needed of course, but happy because she didn't let it get her down—she always seemed to have some sort of plan.

He quietly cleared his throat, looking at her as intently as she was looking at him. "I think you've been working on this Red Gardenia piece for too long."

"How do you mean?"

He shrugged. "Just that you sound like a paranoid homicide detective who sees everyone as a suspect."

"I didn't say you were suspect. But I do think your actions are a bit on the questionable side."

He'd give her that. Another thing Mallory never did was judge you. Oh, sure, she was as cynical—excuse me, realistic—as they came, and she didn't hesitate to share her thoughts with you, but she never made you feel as if she thought she was better than you.

"Why did you start drinking?"

Jack felt his heart stop beating in his chest at the quietly asked question.

Whoa. How did they advance from how he filled his days to why he started drinking?

He avoided her gaze. "You already had your one question."

But as he looked into her eyes, he had a sinking sensation that she wasn't going to let go of this one.

7

FOR AS LONG AS Mallory had known Jack, she'd always pondered what could have made him turn to drink. He always seemed so in control of his environment, so at peace with the world. It boggled the mind to think that he'd once given that peace and control over to alcohol.

She watched the expressions flick across his handsome face and knew a moment of pause. Had she gone too far? Then again, it was her stern belief that as long as it didn't involve murder or small children or animals, then there was no such thing as too far.

Then why hadn't she asked him before now?

Her throat tightened. She hadn't asked him before now because she'd sensed that the reasons behind his alcoholism ran deep and hard and that to ask him to talk about it would be tantamount to handing him a rope and showing him a tree.

For all the experience she'd racked up in life, she was still in the dark when it came to addictive personalities. What made someone drink? Stick a needle in their arm? Take a drug that smelled like, tasted like and essentially had the same effects as rat poison? The question had always perplexed her. For the most part, life was, well, life, and it was fine just the way it was. Sure, some pretty crappy stuff was known to happen, but didn't it happen to everyone? Then what made some people reach for an emotional escape via pharmaceutical or other means, while others just coped?

She frowned at the direction of her thoughts, realizing she'd been thinking in the third person because even she had been reluctant to apply them directly to Jack. It was more than the fear of prying, it was her own fear that she'd say something to hurt him, as she was known to do without even realizing she was doing it.

But she wanted to know. Longed to get that forbidden look inside the shadow of Jack's heart beyond his standard line, "Well, with a name like Jack Daniels, what would you have me do?"

Unfortunately she didn't think she was going to get that glimpse. Because she could already see Jack readying himself to bolt. Probably straight for the door and as far away from her uncomfortable question as he could.

Still, she couldn't bring herself to retract that question, no matter how much her needing to know the information smelled of relationship and emotional commitment. She shoved her Five Year Rule aside and concentrated solely on Jack. Because she suspected he needed that. Because she *knew* she needed it.

When he remained silent, she restrained herself from pushing the issue. She'd thought if she gave him space, he'd tell her in his own time and on his own steam. She was beginning to see that Jack offered nothing up unless he was coerced.

For a guy who wanted more out of their relationship, he was an emotional cripple. She was coming to understand that now and was fascinated with the juxtaposition.

Jack started to get up from the couch.

Mallory knew an instant of regret and letdown. He was going to avoid the question.

He came to stand in front of her. He didn't say anything. Merely brushed the hair back from her cheek. "I think that's enough for one night, don't you? You look like you need some sleep."

Screw sleep, Mallory wanted to say, but bit her tongue.

"What time do you want me to pick you up in the morning?"

She tilted her head to look up at him. "Does that mean the…sex thing is off?"

The sides of his sexy mouth turned up in a semi-grin. "Nope. It just means that tomorrow's open for me and I'd like to help you out."

She smiled at him. Had anyone ever looked out after her the way Jack Daniels did?

If only she didn't feel like he needed something more than she could give him, that might have been enough.

MALLORY HAD NOT ONLY managed to drag herself out of bed by eight o'clock the next morning, she felt, well, okay about it.

Strange, definitely strange.

"Pass the sticky buns, please," she said to Reilly who had just put a plate of them on their table just out of her reach.

Layla, Reilly and Jack all turned to stare at her.

"What?" she asked, wondering how many times a day she found herself saying that.

Layla shook her head. "Nothing. It's just that... well, usually you don't ask."

Mallory twisted her lips. "You're right. I don't know what's gotten into me." She leaned over and snatched up one of the buns, her mouth watering just holding the sweet concoction.

"You know, you should probably give some thought to eating a little healthier," Layla said quietly.

"I'm just glad to be eating," Mallory said.

The friends were looking at her again.

"What?" she said around a full mouth.

Jack cleared his throat while Reilly smiled and Layla folded her napkin.

"Oh, nothing. It's just that that brings us to why we asked you to come this morning," Layla said.

Mallory chased the roll with a long sip of hot, sugary, creamy coffee. Ah, heaven. "You mean we're not here for our regular gossip session?"

"Nope," Reilly said.

Mallory put down her roll. "And we're not here to discuss where you guys stand in the various stages of breakup?"

Layla's cheeks colored the slightest bit while Reilly frowned so deeply Mallory was half-afraid the grimace would never go away.

"Sorry. I didn't mean that."

What she'd meant to say was that she hadn't intended for it to hurt. She'd been trying to poke fun. Instead she'd jabbed at gaping wounds.

Too soon for humor, she guessed.

Layla shifted on the stool as she crossed her legs. She wore a skirt that skimmed her legs above the knees—something she never would have worn before meeting Dr. Sam Lovejoy—and she looked every part the sexy woman and competent doc. "Actually, Mallory, we're here to discuss you."

Mallory nearly choked on her bun. "What?"

But this time she'd expressed the word in a decidedly different way. Instead of exasperated, it was more surprised.

"Me?" She looked at each of them one by one. Jack was staring into the coffee cup he held in both hands, Reilly was smiling to herself and Layla was taking something out of her purse. An envelope, she realized. She slid it across the table so it lay in front of Mallory. It had her name neatly written across the front.

"What, is this an early birthday present?"

She'd be twenty-five in mid-January. But this couldn't be about that. They usually bought her T-shirts to add to her growing collection. In fact, she had on the one Reilly bought her last year, the saying considerably tamer than what she preferred. It featured a skeleton wearing a wide-brimmed hat sitting on a park bench and read Waiting For Mr. Right across the top.

This was the first time she'd worn it. And she wasn't all that clear on why she'd chosen it this morning except that she'd felt somehow...mellower.

Which didn't make any sense. Because given Jack's evasive maneuvers last night, shouldn't she be more agitated?

Still, all she could think about was that he'd brought her food, apologized for the previous night, then revealed more about himself than she likely realized.

And none of it had anything to do with sex.

Stranger yet.

"Open it and see," Reilly said.

Uh-oh. Her friend looked a little too excited than Mallory was comfortable with just then.

With slow, controlled movements she turned the envelope over then opened the flap.

"This, um, looks suspiciously like a check," she said so quietly she nearly didn't hear herself.

She flipped it over then slid it back toward Layla. "I don't accept charity."

"You didn't even look at it!" Reilly said.

"And I'm not going to." The food Mallory had eaten churned in her stomach. She was not a charity case. In fact, she couldn't even remember if she'd told her friends about the financial problems she was currently experiencing.

Her gaze traveled to Jack.

"I'm going to go get some napkins," he said and started getting up from the table.

Mallory snaked out a hand and slapped it on his arm. "Just a minute, Daniels."

Layla sat forward. "This isn't what you think it is, Mallory."

"Oh, yeah? Then someone explain to me what it is, because right now I feel like I should be standing on the street corner holding a sign saying I'll work for food."

Reilly snapped to. "We want to invest in your documentary."

That caught her up short. "What?"

Jack held her gaze, but didn't say anything.

"And this has nothing whatsoever to do with the eviction notice you saw on my door the other day, Layla? Or my car that bit the dust? Or the fact that I make a meal out of sticky buns whenever we get together?"

"Nope," Layla answered without blinking. "It has to do solely with The Red Gardenia."

Oh, hell. Mallory suddenly, inexplicably felt near tears.

Had anyone ever done something so nice for her? Oh, sure, she heard what they were telling her. That they were investing in the film, not her. But if they were interested in investing in a film, she would be the last anyone would willingly seek out. Her last documentary on border laws got picked up by a total of five PBS stations in Southern California, Arizona and Utah.

No, they were doing this because they were her friends.

"I can't," she said. The fact that they were her friends made accepting the money impossible.

"I told you this wouldn't work," Jack said.

But Layla apparently wasn't anywhere near giving up. "Look, Mallory, all three of us happen to think you're a damn good filmmaker with huge potential. But I don't think we're going to be able to sell you on that. So how about this? Take this money as a loan, then. Take it because we're your friends, we care about you, and right now we happen to have the money and you don't.''

Reilly cleared her throat. ''Take it, Mall.''

She started to shake her head.

''Look, somewhere down the line our roles might be reversed,'' Layla said. ''It may be you that has the money and one of us who doesn't. Wouldn't you want to help us out?''

''No,'' Mallory said without hesitation.

A moment of silence, then loud laughter.

Mallory was horrified by her answer. What she'd meant was ''No, our roles would never be reversed. Never in a million years.'' That her friends understood that made her feel all syrupy inside.

Layla pushed the envelope back. ''Take it.'' She grasped Mallory's hand and placed it over the envelope. ''This is what friends do, you know.''

Mallory was shaking her head though her hand remained on the envelope. ''I don't know any friends who do this.''

''Then maybe you've been hanging out with the wrong kind of friends,'' Reilly said quietly.

That was it.

Mallory dipped her chin to her chest and quickly tried to blink back the tears that threatened.

''I'll, um, just go get those napkins,'' Jack said again, and this time Mallory let him leave.

She hated to cry.

She never cried.

She didn't want to be crying now.

But, damn it, she couldn't help it.

Then she took out the check and saw the amount. Far more than she would have ever expected. She could pay the cameraman's salary for the past month. Catch up on her rent. Splurge on that trip to Omaha, Nebraska, to shoot footage of Jenny Fuller's family home. The whole nine.

Her fingers started shaking as she put it back inside the envelope then slid it back to Layla again.

Layla moved it back again.

Reilly sighed. "Look, you can give back anything you don't need. But take it, Mall."

Conflicting emotions filled her. One of the rules her mother had filled her head with was "family never loans money to family; friends never loan money to friends. Not if they hope to stay family and friends."

She caught her lip between her bottom teeth. She could make this work. Couldn't she?

She looked at Layla and Reilly and at where Jack talked to Reilly's young niece, Tina, at the counter and she thought that she'd better make it work. Because if she didn't, she'd risk losing the three most important people in her life.

THREE HOURS LATER Jack sat at a table at Benardo's Hideaway with his mother, in the middle of the lunch he'd been dreading since she'd called yesterday morning.

"So that's why your father—and I, of course—think it would be a good idea for you to take up the reins of the Daniels Foundation."

Jack looked around the comfortable restaurant. The reasoning behind his request that he and his mother have lunch here was threefold. First, he'd known she'd hate it. There wasn't enough crystal around to satisfy his mother's snobbish tastes. Second, he'd get a chance to talk to Ben without being too obvious about it. And third, he'd invited Sam to join him there, purposely scheduling the meeting to occur halfway through his lunch with his mother so he'd have a valid excuse for leaving.

He cleared his throat and speared a spinach leaf in his salad. Celia Daniels was well turned out, as usual. She'd probably been to both the hairdresser and the manicurist that morning, and her pink two-piece suit was obviously a designer label. And her makeup…she'd done her usual evasive maneuvers to prevent him from actually making contact with her cheek when he tried to kiss her because Lord forbid he should disturb her makeup in any way.

"I'm not going to head up the foundation, Mother."

She waved her buffed, lotioned, powdered—was she wearing body makeup?—and bejeweled hand. "Nonsense. Both your father and I agree that we've let you go your own way for long enough now. And since you haven't found your path yet, and probably never will, then we'll decide what that path will be for you.''

Jack stared at the woman opposite him, having difficulty believing she'd actually given birth to him. "Is that right?"

"Don't take that tone with me, young man."

He slowly put his fork down, giving up on ceremony and watched as his plate was quickly taken away. He folded his hands on top of the table. "I'm not a young man anymore, Mother, and whatever tone I use is one you deserve."

She pointed a finger at him and started wagging it. "It's that...Woodruff woman, isn't it? That girl we caught in your apartment that morning. She's the reason for this irreverence, isn't she?"

One of the very few times Celia and Charlie Daniels had ever stopped by his apartment unannounced was three months ago at nine o'clock on a Sunday morning. Imagine their surprise when Mallory had opened the door dressed only in one of her T-shirts—it had read Men Are Pigs And I Love Pork—while Jack had been in the shower. Their knocking had startled Mallory out of a deep sleep and...well, things had gone from bad to worse really quickly. Mainly because his parents had refused to even look at Mallory after he came into the room, and made a point of ignoring her completely, even when she'd grumbled an invitation for them to have some coffee with her.

"No, Mallory is not to blame."

"I don't believe you. One so common...well, it's only so long before that commonness begins to rub off on a person."

Common. As though Mallory would never share the rarified air his mother breathed?

Lately it seemed the people with close ties to him were going out of their way to make his life more difficult.

"Thank you for the invitation, Mother, but I'm afraid I'm going to have to decline your generous offer to head the foundation. Truth is, I just don't have the time."

She made a sound of disbelief then sighed heavily. "Well, then, your father and I have decided that your monthly stipends will have to cease."

Jack smiled to himself. He'd been waiting for this day to arrive. And now that it had, he felt a sense of relief so profound he nearly couldn't breathe.

A swath of light cut across the restaurant from the front door. He glanced to find Sam entering. He couldn't have timed it better. He waved to him, then wiped his mouth and put his napkin on the table.

"Do what you must," he told his mother. "My next appointment has just arrived, so if you'll excuse me."

Celia Daniels looked as if her eyeballs might join the snails on her plate. "What?"

She was so shocked she forgot to block his attempt to make contact with her cheek. Although given the amount of makeup and powder he came away with, he wasn't all that certain the alternative was that much better. "Please, continue with your meal. The food is excellent here and I've got the check. I'll call you later in the week."

He turned, greeted Sam, then quickly led the esteemed doc toward the bar and away from his mother.

8

"SO, HERE WE ARE AGAIN," Sam Lovejoy said, downing half a glass of club soda, then setting it back on the bar.

Jack absently rubbed his chin, knowing Layla's jilted groom was speaking metaphorically rather than literally, because he and Sam had never met without Layla being present. No, rather Sam was referring to the night Jack first met him at Layla's place and the two men had gone outside so Jack could catch a cigarette. Jack had essentially asked Sam what his intentions were toward Layla and Sam had told him he never wanted to hurt her.

Well, that had obviously changed. Although Jack wasn't entirely clear on how Sam was to blame.

He glanced over his shoulder where his mother had vacated their table shortly after he had, apparently deciding the food wasn't enough to keep her there.

Sam started shaking his head. "I thought Layla had accepted that being a cosmetic surgeon came first, and being staff administrator at Trident Medical Center came second. Who would have known she'd blow the way she did when I told her of my intentions to quit Trident and go back into private practice?''

Jack grimaced. ''You could have asked me. I would have told you she'd blow.''

Sam squinted at him. ''But it doesn't make any sense.''

''Did you include her in the decision-making process?''

''What?''

Jack shrugged, nursing an extra-large cup of coffee. ''Did you tell her you were even considering the move? Or did you just come out and tell her the decision was made?''

Sam still didn't seem to be following him.

Jack glanced toward the kitchen door, somewhere behind which Ben Kane stood. The restaurant owner and Reilly's very recent ex-boyfriend had promised to join them in a few minutes, but Jack was getting the sneaking suspicion that Ben was avoiding them. Not that he could blame the guy. Just as Layla and Reilly were still in hurt mode, the men they had dumped were still in anger mode. Well, Ben was, anyway. Sam just looked plain dumbstruck.

''I'll be back in a minute,'' he said, pushing from his stool.

It actually took him five minutes to pry Ben from

where he pretended to be busy at work with invoices back in his office.

"Shall we take this to a booth?" Jack asked.

Ben motioned toward a corner one that was open and Jack led the way, the other two men reluctantly following.

Of course, Jack really didn't know what he was doing either. He wasn't there to commiserate with them, even though his own love life was basically an unqualified mess at that moment. But if he couldn't help himself, he thought maybe he could help Sam and Ben.

He sat across from them and gave the server a moment to give them water, put a couple plates of appetizers on the table, then ask them if they wanted anything else.

All three of them waved her away, preoccupied with their thoughts.

"You guys look like hell." Jack said, having decided to start with stating the obvious.

And they did look bad. Sam looked like he hadn't slept in a month and the brackets around Ben's mouth were so deep Jack wondered if they might be permanent.

"Yeah, tell me something we don't know," Ben said, sitting back and grumbling under his breath.

"Women," Sam said. He'd upgraded to a beer and was peeling the label from the sweaty bottle. "Can't live with them, can't kill them."

That got a chuckle from Ben while Jack merely grinned. He thought he recalled seeing that saying on one of Mallory's T-shirts, though her version had been referring to men.

He idly wondered what she was doing right then. He'd dropped her back home after she'd reluctantly taken the money they'd offered her. He'd waited around to see if she needed him but she'd immediately gotten on the phone to call her cameraman and had seemed to forget he existed. He couldn't help thinking that her determination to succeed had doubled, probably as a result of being responsible for her friends' money. He'd tried to ask her if she was going to pay her rent that morning and she'd waved him away, leaving him a little concerned that she'd get so wrapped up in making the documentary that she'd forget about everything else.

Him included.

"So," Sam said, having completed the label-removing process. "What was it you were saying about decision making?"

It took Jack a moment to backtrack to their earlier conversation. Oh, yeah. "Okay, here's the deal," he said, looking at both of them and leaning forward in his booth. "Women—especially Layla and Reilly—like to be included in the decision-making process, not have the decisions made for them." He pointed at Sam. "When you just came out to say, one night before your wedding of all times, that you were returning to private practice, the news had come so far out of left field that Layla was knocked for a loop. Did you even breathe a word to her about the possibility beforehand?''

Sam shrugged and turned his hands palms up. "She knew I hated firing people at the Center. And the senior partner's continued monopolization of my time outside work was a constant source of bother for both of us.''

"But did you say 'Hey, Layla, you know I've been thinking about quitting' at any point?''

Sam sat back, obviously trying to recall. "I don't know. Maybe.''

"And then again, maybe not,'' Jack finished.

If the guy wasn't so nice, Jack would hate him. Sam Lovejoy was poster boy material. And Ben Kane hadn't exactly fallen off the ugly tree himself. Women gravitated toward both men like they were the only two available on the entire continent.

"Damn,'' Ben said, running his hands over his face, seeming to get the point without Jack walking him through it. Asking Reilly to close down her shop and join him at the restaurant had been a very bad idea. Probably even worse than Sam leaving Layla out of his decision. "It never even occurred to me to include Reilly in my thought processes. Of course, I also meant for it to be a surprise, you know? I got the sign made up and everything.''

"What sign?'' Sam asked.

Jack realized that the moment Layla had called things off Sam had been cut off from the rest of the friends. "Ben proposed they rename Benardo's Hideaway Ben and Reilly's."

Sam stared at Ben. "Uh-oh."

Ben nodded. "You can say that again."

"Strange how we can see that train coming for someone else but not ourselves," Jack grumbled.

Both men looked at him.

"Jack, ole boy," Ben said. "Sounds like you have a few women problems of your own. Make us feel better and dump."

Jack shook his head. "I promised I wouldn't."

"Wouldn't what?" Sam repeated.

"Dump. You know, share what's going on."

Ben was considering him closely. Too closely. "So that means you're seeing someone we both know."

Jack's gaze snapped to his.

Ben merely grinned. "So how long have you and Mallory been doing the mattress rumba?"

MALLORY CLIMBED FROM Harris's fifteen-year-old cargo van and shaded her eyes from the slanting late afternoon sun with her hand. The magic hour. The hour right before sundown when shadows lengthened and the sunlight took on a hazy, purplish hue.

She shuddered. Every time she visited the scene

of the murder, she got the ultimate creeps. Mainly because everything looked so benign, so normal. Twenty-five years ago the residential subdivision surrounding her had been little more than an empty lot, the first stage of the subdivision having been built a few years before that. It had stood only a block away from where the body had been found.

Where Jenny's naked body wrapped in a plain wool blanket had been dumped.

Forensic science hadn't been nearly as sophisticated back then as it was now. The body had been shipped back home to Nebraska and cremated because the family hadn't been able to stand the thought of Jenny being without feet and certain body parts.

Earlier Mallory had gotten another hour of footage of Coco Cabana sitting in a diner as Mallory interviewed her, Harris the cameraman taping. Behind Coco, Sunset Boulevard was visible through the diner windows and across the street you could just make out the apartment complex—little more than a flophouse—where The Red Gardenia had stayed during her brief time in L.A.

"Mall?"

"Hmm?" She turned to look at Harris who had the camera hefted on top of his right shoulder and was adjusting the angle. "Oh, yeah." She looked across the street behind her. "I want you to start from over there. Pan the overall area. Stay away from the numbers on the curb as much as you can for editing purposes. Then zoom in on this area here,'' she indicated the yard in front of her, in about the same spot the body had been found. There were no cars in the short driveway so she hoped that meant nobody was home and wouldn't mind their shooting there. The last time she'd been out here a neighbor had come shrieking down the street at them, threatening to call the cops. ''Let the dead rest in peace,'' she'd said.

Mallory wondered how there could ever be peace in The Red Gardenia's case when her killer had never been found.

She heard her cell phone ring in the front of the van and reached in to get it. ''Hello?''

''I can't believe you never said anything!''

Mallory pulled the phone back to look at the display. Reilly.

She covered her other ear with her hand and started walking away from the van looking for a quieter spot. ''What? Never said anything about what?''

She heard a loud whistle. She looked to find Harris waving her out of the way of his shot.

She gave him a thumbs-up and hurried in the opposite direction.

''About you and Jack going at it behind Layla's and my back, that's what!''

Mallory froze in the middle of the sidewalk, right

in front of the spot where Jenny had been found. Oh my God, oh my God, oh my God.

"I don't know what you're talking about," she lied.

"Do you want me to get this shot or not?" Harris yelled.

Mallory waved for him to be quiet, not really registering his words.

"I want you at Sugar 'n' Spice within the hour."

Mallory looked around. "I'm out on a shoot."

"I don't care if you're on the friggin' moon, Mallory Woodruff. I want you and Jack here in sixty minutes. Now fifty-nine."

Mallory wanted to ask "or what" but restrained herself because she was afraid of what the answer might be.

Then Reilly hung up.

Mallory's brows shot up as she stared at the silent cell. Had Reilly really just hung up on her?

Yep, she realized, she had.

And, oh boy, was there ever going to be hell to pay.

HAD IT REALLY BEEN ONLY that morning that they'd all been gathered to invest in Mallory's documentary? Yes, Jack realized, it had. He only wished the atmosphere were the same. As it stood now, Layla and Reilly were staring at him as if he were evil incarnate and he felt like rushing for the door. The same door Mallory would be walking through any moment.

He dry-washed his face with one hand. Who would have thought guys couldn't keep secrets any better than women couldn't? Okay, that wasn't a fair statement. But either Sam or Ben had spilled the beans following their conversation earlier. The only question that remained was, which one?

He cleared his throat and gripped his coffee cup. "So," he said, directing his words toward Layla. "Are you and Sam making a move toward reconciliation?"

"I haven't talked to Sam."

Ah, so Ben was the guilty party. Just wait until he saw the guy again.

"So you and Ben are talking again," he said to Reilly.

She merely glared at him.

Damn. This was going to be uglier than he feared.

He knew he and Mallory should have told them before they found out this way. Nothing good ever came from keeping secrets. Especially not of this nature.

He caught movement through the window and watched as Mallory climbed from Harris's van, shouldered her backpack, then knocked on the door. Reilly got up to open the door. She'd put the closed sign on the shop the instant Jack had walked in a short while ago.

"What's up, guys?" she asked breezily although he noticed the wary look in her light brown eyes.

Jack shrugged and neither Layla nor Reilly answered her. Reilly retook her seat and waited for Mallory to sit down. Which took a while. She shrugged the backpack off and put it on her chair, looking through the contents.

"You won't believe the fantastic footage I got today. And I managed to get through to James Earl Jones's agent to discuss the terms for him to narrate. Can you imagine? Darth Vader, in the flesh."

"Mallory?" Layla said in an even voice.

"Hmm?" Mallory looked up from her bag.

"Sit down and shut up."

Mallory blinked at Layla several times then grimaced. With a heavy sigh she dropped the bag to the floor and did as requested. But instead of looking at the other two women at the table, she busied herself with filling the empty coffee cup in front of her from a carafe, then started adding her usual tons of sugar and cream.

Reilly grabbed the sugar bowl and moved it out of reach while Mallory still had her spoon up in the air.

"Talk," Layla said.

They were both looking at Mallory, thank God. Which let Jack off the hook. At least temporarily.

"About what? You guys are the ones that called

this damn meeting,'' Mallory muttered, slanting Jack a murderous look.

He put his hands out palms up and shrugged. ''Don't look at me. I didn't say anything.''

''No,'' Reilly agreed. ''But you should have. Instead I had to find out from Ben on the phone an hour ago.''

''You reconciled with Ben?'' Mallory asked, a transparent attempt to change the subject.

''We're talking,'' Reilly said, tightlipped.

''Yeah, well, that much is obvious,'' Mallory said under her breath. ''And it looks like you two aren't the only ones.''

''Hey,'' Jack said, ''I didn't have to say anything. Ben figured it out without my having to say a word.''

Mallory made a face. ''Which just made it easier on you, didn't it, Jack?''

Layla held up a hand. ''Hey, hold up here. I don't care who said what to whom when. I want to know why you two lied to us for starters.''

''Starters?'' Mallory repeated.

Reilly nodded. ''Yes. Then you're going to have to fill in the rest of the blanks.'' She started ticking items off on her fingers. ''For example, when did you two start seeing each other? How serious is this? What were you thinking, for God's sake?''

Mallory took a long sip from her coffee then grimaced. Apparently there wasn't enough sugar. She reached across and fought Reilly for the sugar bowl. ''Do you want an answer or not?'' she snapped. Reilly nodded. ''So give me the sugar then. I need all the help I can get.''

Jack sighed heavily then sat back on his stool. ''For the record, I wanted to tell you guys.''

Now all three women looked like they wanted to kill him.

Great. A guy couldn't win for losing.

''I don't know why you two are getting so worked up,'' Mallory said, testing her coffee again then looking satisfied. ''There really isn't anything to tell. Not anymore.''

Jack flinched at the utter silence.

''What's that supposed to mean?''

Mallory shrugged. ''Just that Jack and I aren't having sex anymore.''

Layla nearly spewed the contents of her own cup.

''Is that shocking to you?'' Mallory asked. ''That Jack and I have been having sex. Almost from the word go?''

''Since the four of us met three years ago?'' Reilly asked, her mouth agape.

Mallory nodded. ''We had our first one-night stand the very same night.''

Layla glared at Mallory. ''The same day the three of us swore we wouldn't go after Jack because our friendship was more important to us than sex?''

Mallory had the decency to look a little ashamed.

"It wasn't something I planned, exactly. Sex with Jack, I mean. And when it happened...well, there wasn't much I could do about it, was there? And it was just the one night."

And then the night three months later. And again a few months after that.

"But there were other nights."

Mallory rolled her eyes. "What, do you want an entire accounting?"

"Yes," Layla and Reilly said at the same time.

"Tough. Because you're not going to get one." Mallory sat forward. "It should be enough to know that it's over."

Silence again.

Jack felt somewhat relieved that the bulk of the anger had been directed toward Mallory, though he supposed he probably should have jumped in to protect her more. He was beginning to feel as if he'd just fed her to the lions.

Then again, if Mallory had listened to him and they had told Layla and Reilly about what was happening between them, they wouldn't be facing this right now.

She deserved to get growled at a bit—if just because she'd screwed up what had been a perfectly fantastic sex life.

He began to get up. "It doesn't look like you guys really need me, so if you don't mind, I'll just be going now."

"Sit down," Reilly and Mallory said simultaneously.

He sat.

Damn.

"God, you can be such a coward," Mallory said.

"*He's* a coward?" Layla asked. "He wanted to tell us. It's you who didn't want us to know. Why, Mallory?"

"Why?" she asked with raised brows. "Well, duh. Look at how upset you guys are now. And we're not even having sex anymore." She shook her head. "I knew exactly this was going to happen."

Silence settled over the table as everyone mulled over what had been said, and what had gone unsaid. Jack lifted his cup only to discover he'd already drunk all the contents. He reached to find the carafe empty. His movements provided the only sounds in the room.

"Why?" Layla asked.

Jack looked from her to Mallory.

"Why what?" Mallory asked.

"Why aren't you and Jack seeing each other anymore?"

9

THIS WAS ALL JUST TOO much for Mallory. One minute she was filming some of the best footage she'd ever taken in her life, the next she was being dragged through the entire three hundred and fifty years of the Spanish Inquisition.

What really stunk was that she was no longer even doing the nasty deed that she was getting the third degree for.

"Why?" Layla repeated. "Why did you two stop seeing each other?"

Had the doctor gone daft in the head? First she was upset that she and Jack were having sex and now she was upset that they weren't?

Mallory reached for her bag. "Does anyone have any aspirin?"

"I'll get some," Reilly said, getting up from the table. "But don't say a word until I get back."

"I wouldn't dream of it," Mallory muttered.

She stared at Jack.

Lily-livered Jack who looked more anxious than a turkey the day before Thanksgiving.

He gave her one of his half grins. The kind that

made her stomach bottom out and made her itch to tackle him to the floor and ride him all night long.

He didn't look the least bit concerned about what was happening. In fact, he appeared a little pleased. But that wasn't possible because he was being grilled just as much as she was. For him to be enjoying this meant...

She widened her eyes. Why that sneaky little dog. This was what he had wanted all along, wasn't it? After all, he was the one who had issued the ultimatum. He was also the one who had let slip to Sam and Ben that the two of them had been involved.

Incredible! He was enjoying watching her get raked over the coals by Layla and Reilly. And he was probably looking forward to hearing her explain why they were over, considering she'd been to blame for their breakup.

Breakup? What breakup? They'd been having sex, not dating.

She shook her suddenly-throbbing head. This whole fiasco was growing more confusing with each passing second.

"Here."

Reilly handed her a couple of aspirin and a glass of water.

Mallory easily swallowed the pills then sat back. She met Jack's gaze, taking in the sexy smug look there, then said, "Actually, I think Jack's the better person to explain why we're no longer having sex. Well, that is if oral sex isn't sex. If it isn't, then the last time we had sex was at your rehearsal dinner.''

Layla gaped at her then Jack, her pale skin turning a sickly ashen color.

Mallory stared at her. ''What? A little too much information for you, Layla? You didn't think Jack and I had stuck to the missionary position, did you?''

Reilly threw her head back and howled with laughter.

Mallory cracked a smile of her own. Laughter was good. Laughter meant they had made a U-turn down inquisition alley and were finding their way back to normalcy.

Whatever that constituted.

''Oral sex is sex,'' Layla said then cleared her throat, as if unable to believe she'd said it.

Mallory gave Jack an ''I told you so'' look.

''A blowjob is not sex,'' Jack argued. ''A blowjob is foreplay.''

Mallory nodded then stopped and shook her head. ''Oral sex is foreplay when actual sex follows afterward. Actual sex did not follow the night before last.''

Reilly shifted in her stool, apparently more comfortable with the topic than Layla was. Curious, considering Layla was the doctor. Maybe she was just too close to her subjects in this particular case.

"I always thought sex was the mutual sharing of pleasure," she said.

Mallory raised her brows at Jack.

"Mall enjoys giving head," he said thoughtfully.

This time Reilly squeaked then held up her hands. "Okay, I think I just joined Layla in the TMI area." She shook her head. "So do either of you plan to answer Layla's original question sometime soon?"

Mallory flapped a hand in Jack's direction. "Be my guest, Jack. You know, seeing as we'd still be having sex if it weren't for your stupid ultimatum."

Layla still look shell-shocked. "You had sex at my rehearsal dinner?"

"Not actually at the dinner, but during it. Namely in a linen closet or something out in the service hall."

Reilly stuck her finger out. "So that's where you guys were." She stared at Jack. "No wonder you were so distracted when you got back."

"Yeah, we both pretty much missed the fireworks," Mall said with a sigh. "We leave, everything's fine, we come back and global war had broken out."

Layla grumbled under her breath, "Sounds like you guys were setting off fireworks all your own. And right under our noses at that." She closed her eyes. "How could we not have seen it?"

"Actually, I suspected," Reilly said quietly.

Mallory, Layla and Jack all gaped at her. "You did not," Layla said.

She smiled. "Yes, I did." She shrugged. "Well, maybe I didn't. But Ben did. He said there was something about the way that Jack looked at Mallory that gave him away."

"So Ben suspected and told you."

"Mmm. But I didn't buy it at first. Until I started noticing the way you two looked at each other."

"Why didn't you say anything?" Layla wanted to know.

Reilly shrugged again. "It wasn't my news to share. Anyway, it's not even news anymore, so what's the difference?"

Layla was looking unhappier by the moment. "The difference is that that makes you just as guilty as the two of them."

"Well, that doesn't make any sense. How can I be guilty when I didn't do anything?"

Layla waved her away. "One sinner at a time." She focused her gaze on Jack. "So spill. Why aren't you two seeing each other anymore?"

Mallory sat back on her stool and crossed her arms. This, she had to hear.

Jack grimaced and gripped his empty coffee cup so hard Mallory was half-afraid he'd shatter it. "Because after we…um, after the rehearsal incident, I told Mallory that unless we told you two, it was over."

Damn. He'd come right to the point without even a bit of sputtering.

And now Layla and Reilly were looking accusingly at her again.

"What?" she barked.

"Is that true? Is that the ultimatum you mentioned?" Layla asked.

Talk about your hemming and hawing. Mallory slowly sipped at her cup of steaming coffee, then deliberately took her time reaching for a sticky bun and licking the syrup from her thumb. "Maybe," she said quietly.

"Excuse me?" Layla said, putting a hand to her ear. "I didn't quite catch that."

Mallory leaned toward her as if to whisper into her ear then shouted, "I said 'maybe'!"

Her friend glared at her.

"Okay, okay, it is, all right? Are you happy now? Jack and I were having phenomenal sex behind your back. He wanted to tell you two about our relationship. My argument was that we didn't have a relationship, we were merely having sex. So he decided that was that and left me high and dry."

Jack's chuckle surprised them all.

He coughed into his hand. "Sorry." He slanted Mallory a devilish glance. "You know I've never left you high and dry before."

She found herself smiling at him, her nipples tightening under her T-shirt. "No, you haven't."

"Eeeuw," Reilly said, pushing from her stool. "If bringing all this out into the open means having to watch you two lick each other's faces, I don't think I can handle it."

"Reilly's right," Layla said. "It's a good thing you two aren't...doing it anymore, because just thinking about the two of you being intimately involved is like thinking of my sister and brother going at it."

"You're an only child, Layla," Mallory reminded her.

"So it's what I think I'd feel."

Mallory looked at Jack, resisting the urge to grab his knee under the table. "Sounds...wicked."

"Twisted is more like it," Reilly said, narrowing her eyes at them. "Are you sure you two aren't having sex anymore?"

Mallory's gaze snapped back to her friend's. "Positive."

"Without a doubt," Jack agreed.

"Good," Layla and Reilly said at once.

Mallory's gaze traveled back to Jack. Hmm... Why did she have the feeling that her being left high and dry was no longer going to be an issue?

JACK PUSHED OPEN THE door to his apartment with his hip. With Mallory plastered against his front, tugging at his shirt and diving for the waist of his jeans, he nearly toppled to the floor.

Oh, yeah. He'd definitely missed this.

Her mouth tasted like coffee and sticky buns and something even sweeter. Funny, at any other time he wouldn't use the word sweet to describe anything even remotely related to Mallory Woodruff. But while her mouth could definitely be wickedly naughty, she tasted sweeter than anything he'd ever had against his tongue. Sweet and tangy and completely intoxicating.

"Dog," she said, catching him when he would have tripped over where Boomer was lying across the foyer.

Jack looked down to find Boomer watching them through hooded eyes, his head resting on his paws, his tail pounding lightly against the polished wood floor.

That's how they'd ended up here, back at his place, rather than Mallory's. Jack had to feed Boomer.

He reluctantly grasped Mallory's shoulders and peeled her from his chest. "Why don't you go crawl into the shower...bed...whatever, while I feed B?"

She smiled up at him. "Are you sure we can't squeeze in a quickie before you feed Boomer?"

Jack knew that there would be nothing quick about what he planned to do to Mallory tonight.

"I'm sure," he said, turning her around then swatting her behind.

She gave him a saucy look over her shoulder then

walked with deliberate sexiness away from him. Jack's gaze was glued to her tight little backside in her jeans. What that woman did to a pair of jeans.

"Come on, B," he said, rushing into the kitchen where he positioned a can of dog grub in the can opener then reached into the pantry to fill his dry food bowl. He forked the food onto a plate, filled the dog's water bowl, then put both down on the floor.

Only Boomer was still lying in the foyer watching him.

Boomer always came when there was food.

Actually, when he thought about it, Boomer usually always rushed Mallory when she came through the door.

He walked over to the dog, felt his nose, then ran his hands down over his old flanks. He didn't feel hot and didn't flinch at his probing.

Jack stood back and looked down at him. "Come on, boy. Dinner's on."

Finally, Boomer lumbered to his feet and slowly sauntered to the kitchen.

Jack knew a moment of pause.

"Jack?" Mallory's lilting voice reached out to him from the other room.

He checked to make sure Boomer was eating, then started in the direction of his bedroom.

MALLORY SHIVERED, having stripped down to nothing but her naughty underwear. She was crouched on all fours in the middle of Jack's bed, her bottom pointing high up in the air. She planned for that to be the first thing he saw. And in her leopard print thong, she knew that if he was harboring any doubts, they'd fly straight out the window the moment he saw her.

There was only so much a man could resist, after all. And knowing the way Jack felt about her bottom…well, she knew she held all the cards tonight. And she planned to play every last one of them for all the dough in the pot.

"Damn, but you've got a great ass."

Mallory piled her curly dark hair to the other side of her head and gave him a come-hither look over her shoulder. "Do you think?" She gave a little wiggle just to entice him further.

He was nodding as he pulled his T-shirt over his head, his gaze zoomed in on her bottom. "Oh, yeah."

Mallory arched her back so that her bottom was high up in the air and the tips of her breasts skimmed against the silken sheets. "And what do you want to do to it, Jack?"

His surprised gaze flicked to her face. "As in?"

She reached back and gave an experimental smack to her left cheek. "Do you want to spank it? After all, I've been a very naughty girl."

She heard his low, primal growl as he shut the

door. Within two blinks he'd stripped down and was kneeling on the bed behind her...right where she wanted him to be.

"I don't know...do you want to be spanked?" he rasped.

Mallory wiggled her bottom again. "I might be interested in a love tap or two."

She'd never, ever done something so blatantly subversive before in bed. This was the new millennium, after all. And it wasn't all that long ago when women fought for the right not to be beaten down, both physically and emotionally.

And here she was now tempting Jack to spank her.

A shiver of sheer arousal worked its way down her spine and over her skin, making her wonderfully aware of every part of her body.

Well, maybe not a full-out spanking. But the thought of his hand lightly branding her made her so wet her panties were drenched.

But rather than a tap, she felt his fingers skim over the curve of her backside from the top of her leg to the small of her back, then down again. She strained backward, trying to force him to touch places that clamored for his attention even more, but he ignored her efforts, focusing on her bottom with the fascination of a man following the lines of an exquisite sculpture.

Only at that moment Mallory didn't want to be

revered. She wanted to be taken. Roughly. Fully. With absolutely no holds barred.

"Hold still," he said.

Mallory hadn't even been aware she was moving until her fabric-covered cleft met with his long, hard arousal. "I can't," she said.

He grasped her bottom, his fingers denting her flesh. "Try harder."

She didn't want to try harder. She wanted him. Now.

She pressed farther back so that his erection was sandwiched between her swollen folds. He groaned and gripped her hips tighter.

Mallory would have smiled except she was too consumed with need to do anything but seek the wild meeting of their bodies.

She felt a light, stinging smack to her right cheek and gasped.

Wow.

"Hold still, naughty girl, and take your punishment," he said, this time more tightly.

She did the complete opposite. She wriggled her hips, drawing her heat along his long, thick length.

Another smack. But this time she'd been prepared for it and her reaction was instant climax.

A deep moan eased from her throat and she pressed her ultra-sensitive nipples more firmly against the mattress, enjoying the convulsing and contracting of her vaginal and stomach muscles.

"Holy cow," she whispered long moments later.

She heard Jack's quiet chuckle. "Not exactly the words I would have used, but, yeah."

Mallory collapsed to the mattress, incapable of holding herself up.

"Oh, no," Jack murmured. "We're nowhere near finished, baby."

She swallowed hard. "I was hoping you'd say that."

Jack turned her over and swept her panties from her, tossing them to the far corner. Mallory pushed nearer the headboard to give him room, but he apparently didn't want it as he grabbed her legs behind the knees and dragged her so that her vulva rested against his pulsing length. He'd already put on a condom. She was barely able to pull in a breath before he sank into her to the hilt, filling her in every way it was possible to fill a woman.

She stretched her neck and moaned, loving the feel of him so deep inside her. In that one moment she felt complete. Whole. Like she was no longer alone in the world but part of something larger than herself. Bigger than them both.

Jack smoothed his fingers up over her hips and over her ribs so he could cup her breasts from underneath, gently squeezing them through her lacy bra. He bent and fastened his mouth over one straining tip, his erection still inside her. Mallory grabbed his shoulders as he worked the tip of his tongue into the upper part of her demi bra and coaxed out her nipple, not stopping until he pulled it deep into his mouth.

Fire swept over her limbs, filling her with restless energy.

"Forget the breasts," she ordered him, jerking her hips up. "Make love to me."

She caught her breath. She'd never used those words before. Sex was the usual word of choice.

If Jack's stillness as he slowly pulled back and stared down at her was any indication, he'd also caught the slip.

But thankfully he didn't say anything.

Rather, he began moving, his arousal stroking her slick muscles with slow deliberation. Making her back come off the bed, stealing her breath, making her skin damp, while she held his gaze unblinkingly.

He had the most beautiful eyes she'd ever seen. When he looked at her, she felt like she was the most important thing in the world. The person who mattered most to him.

And she felt a love so consuming that it scared her to death.

"Talk to me, Mallory. Tell me what you're feeling," he whispered, running his tongue along the shallow valley between her breasts then up to her jaw.

"I'm feeling like I'm going to explode," she

whispered, moaning when he filled her to the hilt with one smooth stroke.

"And?"

And what? What did he want her to tell him? That she was so wide open to him that she didn't know whether to laugh or cry? That her emotions were such a jumbled mess she couldn't make sense out of her own thoughts? Or that if he dared try to issue any more ultimatums she'd have to kill him because the thought of going without him for even a day was almost too much to bear?

"And..." She swallowed hard. "And I'm feeling like I never want this to end."

His pupils had long ago claimed the brown of his eyes. She drowned in them as he drew closer to her and pressed his mouth against hers. She kissed him slowly, languidly at the same time that her stomach began shaking in pre-climax.

Then she let loose, giving herself over to the sensations ripping through her body with no reservations, no inhibitions, and absolutely no worry about what she should or should not be allowing to happen.

10

"The wedding's back on."

Jack rubbed the pads of his fingers against his closed eyelids and tried to focus on what Layla was saying to him on the phone. But focusing on anything at 7 a.m. wasn't easy. Not when Mallory had her sweet little bottom pressed against his side, her soft snores telling him she hadn't even heard the phone ring on the nightstand, and certainly hadn't heard him answer it.

"What?" he croaked.

"Are you still in bed?" Layla asked, sounding happier than she had in a long time. Well, in a few days anyway.

"Yeah," he said, squinting at the alarm clock. He hadn't set it the night before. By this time he was usually returning from his run or on his second cup of coffee.

"Are you…alone?"

Jack opened his mouth to speak, but nothing came out.

"No. Forget I asked that. I don't want to know."

"What's this about weddings being back on?" he asked.

At the sound of the word "weddings," Mallory snapped instantly awake then jackknifed to a sitting position, her breasts gloriously bare in the dim light filtering in through the window. "What, what, what?" she asked sleepily.

Jack moved the phone to the other side of his head, listening as Layla said, "Not weddings, Jack. One wedding. Namely mine. To Sam."

He found himself grinning. "Glad to hear you two came to your senses."

"Yeah," Layla said in a wistful way that made him want to ask if *she* was alone. But he didn't because he wasn't going to open that door, either. "We were up all night talking. In fact, Sam just left to see to the opening of his new practice."

Jack's grin widened. He'd bet dollars to doughnuts that talking wasn't all the couple had done.

"Anyway, you and Reilly were the first ones I could think to call," Layla said. "Mallory's probably still sleeping."

"Probably," he admitted, watching as Mallory tried to maneuver herself to listen in on the conversation.

"Anyway, I don't know when, and I don't know where, but be ready to attend a wedding ceremony at a moment's notice."

Jack reached his free hand over and toyed with

Mallory's right nipple. She swatted his hand away and made a face at him.

"You're not going the whole nine yards route this time around?"

"What, have that circus Sharon wanted me to have? No." He heard the soft rustling sound of movement and wondered if she was still in bed as well. "I'm beginning to think that all of this happened because of the stress involved with all that hassle."

"It would be enough to scare away the bravest of souls."

Layla laughed. "Yeah. Maybe. Anyway, if you talk to Mallory before I do, pass on the news, okay?"

Mallory stared at him.

Jack cleared his throat. "Okay, I will."

He clicked the disconnect button then put the cordless back on the night table.

Mallory chewed on her bottom lip for a moment then said, "Why didn't you tell her I was here?"

Jack shrugged. "She said she didn't want to know."

She lifted her brows. "God, you know, I don't think I'll ever be able to figure you out, Jack."

She pulled the top sheet from his legs and wrapped it around herself then began to get up. "Good. That means you'll never get bored."

"That's not the kind of figuring I mean. Surprising me with a trip to Catalina, that's a good surprise. Not telling Layla I was in bed next to you when you made such a big deal out of wanting to tell them about us to begin with...well, that just doesn't make sense."

"Why didn't you take the phone?"

She shrugged, her delectable back to him. "I don't know. It wasn't my place, I guess."

"Mmm. Like you always overly concern yourself with your place," he said and grimaced.

Were they arguing?

Yes, they were definitely arguing.

After a night of fantastic sex.

Jack collapsed back against his pillow thinking he'd never be able to figure out this relationship stuff.

Or were he and Mall still just having sex?

He followed her movements with his eyes as she picked up her clothes from various parts of the room. "Where are you going?"

"Home."

He patted the bed next to him. "It's way before noon. Why don't you come back here?"

She stared at him. "It's Thursday. Don't you have a class or something to get to?"

"Not until ten."

"Well, you'd better get a head start because as slow as you move, you don't want to be late."

Jack winced at the carefully aimed jab. They

were back to the lack of ambition bit again, were they?

He watched her get dressed. She seemed to take extra care not to let him see any of her sweet flesh. Which didn't make sense, because Mallory didn't possess a lick of modesty.

"Are you upset with me?" he asked.

"Upset? Why would I be upset?"

"Because I didn't tell Layla we were together."

She shrugged in a jerky way that told him the gesture was anything but nonchalant. "I don't care what you tell Layla."

Uh-oh.

Jack cleared his throat.

"Anyway, I've got to get going. Harris and I are flying out at eleven this morning to shoot some film of Jenny Fuller's childhood home in Omaha, Nebraska."

"You're going to Nebraska?"

She nodded. "Yeah."

She pulled up her jeans with her back to him and he heard her yank up the zipper.

"When will you be back?"

She shrugged. "Tonight. Tomorrow. Depends on the weather and if we can get the shots we need."

Irrationally, he suddenly regretted that they'd given her the money.

"Then when I get back, I need to take what I have over to the editing studio and have them piece something rough together to take over to the James Foundation to see if I can get full backing. Maybe even distribution.''

''The money we gave you isn't enough?''

She didn't answer him as she put on her socks and her boots.

''Mallory?''

She walked over to the bed, kissed him fully yet coolly on the mouth, then tousled his hair. ''I'll see you when I see you.''

Jack could do little more than watch her go.

I'll see you when I see you? Had she really just said that? Never, ever in all the time they'd been sleeping together had she ever said anything so...chilly before.

He absently scratched his head as he listened to her talk to Boomer in the other room then heard the sound of the front door closing.

Was this her way of paying him back for the other night when he'd left her place after receiving the best blowjob of his life?

No. He didn't think so. While Mallory was outspoken and brash, she wasn't the vengeful type.

Was she?

He forced himself to roll out of bed. At any rate, there wasn't much he could do about it now.

He only wished he knew when he would be able to do something about it. Because it sure looked as though he wouldn't be seeing her for a while.

MALLORY HAD NEVER THOUGHT much of traveling before, but now she absolutely despised it. All the waiting and checking and probing just to hop a three-hour flight to and from a place no one in their right mind would want to bomb. And when the stewardess—oh, excuse me, flight attendant—had gotten snippy with her, Mallory had had to hold her tongue, because nowadays a person could get arrested for expressing an opinion to the glorified flying waitress. What happened to innocent until proven guilty? Now they looked at even her as potential terrorist material because she didn't look or talk like Mrs. Brady from *The Brady Bunch.*

When the ordeal was finally over, she dropped her backpack outside her apartment door and sighed at the yellow slip of paper stapled to the wood. It was 2 a.m. on a weeknight and even this part of L.A. was quiet. Well, except for the second warning eviction notice shouting at her from her door.

She snatched the annoying note from the door, let herself inside, then slammed it after herself.

From the moment she accepted the money she'd determined not to use any of it for personal reasons. Not for her rent, her cell phone bill or to fix her car. No. She'd use every cent for the documentary piece.

She tossed her backpack to her clothes-covered couch then collapsed next to it, her mind zooming with everything that had happened that day. From

Layla's call to Jack that morning, to her disturbing interview with one of Jenny Fuller's neighbors. Just thinking about the woman made her shudder.

"Jenny and my son dated all throughout high school. Arnold fully expected they would marry. But that wasn't good enough for Jenny. Oh, no. She had to go off to Hollywood and break my son's heart."

Mallory had immediately thought that it couldn't have been too serious if Jenny had still been a virgin when she died.

And where was the son now?

The mother had shrugged. "Off in California, somewhere. Not L.A. though. He left home shortly after Jenny did."

Nowhere in her research had she come across any mention of a spurned boyfriend following Jenny to California. Nowhere was there mention of her being seen with a man, or of anyone worthy of note visiting her apartment. Had Jenny known Arnold had followed her? Or had Arnold been stalking her?

Mallory reached into her backpack and took out her handheld notepad, flipping through the pages looking for his full name and any additional information the mother had given her. With any luck, she'd be able to find out where he lived in California and arrange to speak with him.

She folded then straightened the edge of the note paper. She wasn't sure what it was about this one subject that fascinated her so. Sure, she was obsessed to some degree with every project she worked on. But this one...

She tucked the notepad back into her pack. She supposed it might be the similarities between her and Jenny. Jenny had left her hometown to seek a career in Hollywood. Twenty-five years later Mallory had done the same. Of course, their goals once in Tinseltown had been different, but their backgrounds, the motivating factors, had essentially been the same.

"She'd wanted to be Sally Field. Make a difference in movies," Jenny's mother had said.

And Mallory wanted to make documentaries on topics that most people wouldn't touch with a ten-foot pole.

Of course, that's where the similarities ended. Mallory had always been a tomboy and gave no more thought to her appearance than a comb through her hair and a toothbrush to her teeth. Jenny, on the other hand, had been as feminine as they came. She'd had a daily beauty ritual that could pass as a part-time job.

Then there was the detail that Jenny Fuller, aka The Red Gardenia, had been murdered and Mallory, thank heaven, was still very much alive.

She stared at the poster of The Red Gardenia that she had hanging on the opposite wall. It had already become faded and frayed around the edges, but seemed to grow even more so just hanging on Mallory's wall. The tape under the right-hand corner of the paper had ceased working so the edge curled upward. In the dim light, Mallory thought it almost looked like time was trying to fold up on the image, hide it away. But she refused to let the memory of Jenny fade away because this one woman represented the lives and dreams of so many others. Young women who had left everything they had known to come out to L.A. and find a new life for themselves.

Though in Jenny's case, she had found death.

Mallory slid her cell phone from her front pants pocket and checked it for messages. Nothing. She sighed and stuffed it into the front of her backpack. Jack hadn't tried to contact her all day. What did that mean beyond he had taken her at her word and she would see him when she saw him?

This morning while he'd been talking to Layla, she'd grown inexplicably irritated. And the time between then and now hadn't helped her figure out why. After all, she was the one who'd said what they shared was nothing but great sex.

And the sex was still great.

Great? It was mind-blowingly phenomenal.

So, then, what was her problem?

She plucked a T-shirt from the arm of the couch, looked at it, then began folding it. She supposed part of the problem lay in that the rest of her life was such a mess, why wouldn't her relationship with Jack be the same?

Five years. That's what she'd given herself. Five years to make it in L.A. And that time limit was fast approaching. Not only hadn't she made it; she was considerably in the hole.

Before she knew it, she'd folded every last one of the items of clothing on the couch and had them stacked in the laundry basket.

As much as she hated L.A. and all the superficiality that went along with the city, she admitted that the place was a source of endless fascination. The wanna-be actresses from the Midwest still got off buses with stars in their eyes. Still had to battle past pimps and drug dealers just to walk down the street. Young and determined, they'd either read of others who'd made it that way before them, or naively believed they could set a precedent.

But just as the city had its bad side, it also had its good. Magic was still made here. Both in films and in reality. A little known waitress one day could blow up into a million-dollar actress seemingly overnight. The weather was always nice, the sun always seemed to be shining and the very air itself seemed…full of possibilities somehow. Sure, Mallory knew about the smog and that air advisories were issued so frequently she didn't even pay attention to them anymore. And every now and again the earth shook threateningly. And water was a constant source for worry. She only thanked God she didn't have a lawn to water. (Then again, she probably wouldn't have grass anyway.)

But Los Angeles was beautiful in so many ways that she imagined it was very easy to forget to remember how ugly it could be underneath.

Before she knew it, she'd moved on to the files littering the floor, working on them until they were neatly organized and sitting in a stack on the freshly cleaned and dusted dining room table. She straightened and picked up and swept and dusted until she stood in the middle of the apartment barely able to recognize it as her own.

When had she gotten so sloppy?

Oh, yeah. When she'd left home and there was no longer anyone around to harp on her to pick up her clothes.

She crossed her arms. Her mother would be proud.

Which, of course, instantly made her want to mess it all up again. A juvenile reaction to be sure, but she'd learned long ago to take whatever pleasures life threw your way and enjoy them. And being messy just because she knew it would piss off her mom had been one of those pleasures.

Well, that, and she never seemed to have time to clean.

She glanced at her watch. It was three-thirty. And she wasn't tired in the least.

She twisted her lips, wondering if she should call Jack.

No, a quiet voice told her.

But why, she couldn't be sure.

There was a dull clanging sound outside her apartment. Not unusual, given that the majority of the complex inhabitants were either dealers or prostitutes, nighttime was pretty much working time. But for some reason a jolt of fear raced up her spine.

She switched off the light and moved toward the front window. The heavy curtains were drawn, but the outside light showed a crack between them. She stepped to the side of the window and pushed the curtain slowly outward. She couldn't make out anything. Not a person, not a cat, nothing that could have made the sound.

Movement.

Mallory nearly jumped out of her sneakers as a figure craned its neck toward the crack in the middle of the curtains.

Air rushed out of her lungs.

It was Coco.

Mallory switched the light back on then opened the door.

"Shit!" the aging prostitute said, putting a hand over her chest. "You scared the crap out of me."

"Yeah, well, that makes two of us," Mallory said. "You might as well come on in, seeing as sleep isn't an option now."

Coco smiled as she entered. "Sorry if I startled you. It's just that I didn't feel much like working tonight and Candy has someone over." She held up a bottle of tequila. "And I didn't come empty-handed."

Mallory felt like kissing the other woman. "Nothing like a little tequila to make the sandman come."

"You can say that again." Coco stopped in the middle of the room, taking in the neat appearance. "What happened here?"

Mallory was used to getting that response when her place was a mess. "Just thought I'd tidy up a bit."

"A bit? Girl, it looks like you've been possessed by June Cleaver's ghost."

Mallory laughed as she got two juice glasses from the kitchen then sat down next to Coco on the couch.

"You know, with the hours you keep, you should give some thought to hooking for a living."

Mallory wrinkled her nose as she broke the seal on the bottle then poured a healthy shot into each juice glass. She handed one to Coco. "Not my cup of tea. I can only have sex when I'm moved to."

"Money can be a good motivator."

"Not that good."

Coco smiled. "So...how did the trip to Omaha go today?"

The tequila had a bite to it, but it immediately went to work on Mallory's tense muscles. She relaxed a little more into the cushions and sighed. "I don't know. Good, I guess. I got some great footage of where she grew up. And her family was real cooperative." She shrugged. "I think they're still hoping the killer will be brought to justice."

"Mmm. After twenty-five years."

"It's all they've got to hold on to."

"I suppose. But it seems a little unrealistic to me. I mean people are murdered all the time and the killers are never caught."

Mallory nodded.

"Anyway, I just wanted to stop and tell you that I stumbled across the best little sale at Neiman…"

For the next forty-five minutes, Mallory sat through makeover tip after makeover tip, stopping short of letting Coco experiment on her. The contents of the bottle sank lower and lower until Mallory was pleasantly buzzed and could barely hold her head up straight.

She cleared her throat and finally had to interrupt Coco in the middle of her wardrobe critique. "Whoa. There's only so much positive input a girl can take," she said, then yawned. "I'm going to dream I'm on that *Extreme Makeover* show tonight."

Coco laughed then looked at her faux diamond-encrusted watch. "You're right. It is getting late, isn't it?'' She rose fluidly from the couch while Mallory practically had to roll herself off to walk Coco to the door.

Just outside the door, the friendly prostitute turned. ''I hope you can make this documentary fly, Mallory. Jenny deserves it.''

Mallory was silent for a long moment. ''I hope I can, too, Co. I hope I can, too.''

11

JACK SAT STARING AT THE blinking cursor on his computer screen for the third time in as many days. His deadline was quickly coming up and he couldn't seem to take an idea beyond, well, idea stage. In fact, there were a lot of things he couldn't seem to scare up much enthusiasm for lately. Christmas being one of them.

Well, at least one thing had finally come to fruition. He'd received a certified letter from his parents' family attorney first thing this morning. He'd finally, officially, been cut off from the family fortune. His monthly allowance was now history.

He leaned back in his chair and grinned.

Someone on the outside looking in might find his behavior odd. But all he could feel was celebratory. And free. Blissfully, happily free.

For as long as he could remember, he'd lived on his family's dime. Throughout college they'd paid for everything, including getting him into the best fraternity. Then after that they'd got him a swanky apartment just off campus (even though the family house was only a fifteen-minute drive away). And all that time he'd never felt he had to take responsibility for anything. Not financially. Not for his behavior. Not for himself, period.

"Cut the cords," his AA sponsor had told him after they'd been meeting for a few weeks.

Jack had squinted at him, convinced the guy had gone insane. Everyone he knew lived off their family's money. Hell, his father even lived off the money his father before had left him, and so on and so on.

"Until you start taking responsibility for yourself, then you'll never take yourself seriously."

The words had made sense. So he'd asked his father to cut off his very generous monthly allowance.

Instead his father had doubled it.

But that didn't mean he had to spend it. Rather than depositing the checks in his checking account, he'd arranged to have them direct deposited into a savings account, determined to forget about it. He'd lived on his own steam ever since, working first at various newspaper jobs, writing short stories for some women's magazines under a female pseudonym, then he'd landed the gig at *L.A. Monthly.* He'd begun teaching for kicks, and to freshen up his own skills as a journalist.

As for teaching how to write fiction...

He pushed his chair back and opened his bottom desk drawer, staring at the two-and-a-half unpublished novels there, books he'd written to pass the time when he'd first sobered up. He had filled three thick journals in quick succession… They were something into which he'd poured all his conflicting emotions, trying to make sense out of his thoughts. He'd found it helped to create characters and give them his problems and see what they did with them. It had been therapeutic.

More, he'd found he liked disappearing into the fictional worlds he created. Just as he'd once loved to read, he'd learned to love to write.

He closed the drawer. Then one morning he'd woken up and just simply stopped writing. It was as though he'd exorcised himself of the alcohol demon and could go forward without his crutches.

But recently his mind had been turning back to those books more and more.

He stared at the blinking cursor. Of course, none of that was helping him write his column.

He leaned backward and stared at the silent phone in the kitchen. Was Mallory back from Omaha yet? Did she miss him as much as he missed her?

He hadn't realized how very much he did miss her until that very moment.

Actually, it wasn't exactly that he missed her. They had just been together the previous morning. It was the idea that there was nothing concrete, no commitment to bind them, that bothered him more than anything. Made his longing for her manifest itself into missing her.

"How do you like that?" he said to himself.

Boomer lifted his head and whimpered.

Jack dropped his hand and scratched the dog behind his big floppy ears.

"WE'RE GETTING MARRIED."

Mallory tried to shake the cobwebs from her head as she tugged the sheet down from over her eyes. "Layla?" she asked into the phone.

"No, silly, it's Reilly."

Mallory squinted at her alarm clock. 10 a.m. She groaned and slid back down under the covers.

Was it possible to hear too much good news? First Layla had reconciled with Sam and now Reilly was going to marry Ben.

She groaned again.

"Mall?"

She moved the cell so she could speak into it. "What?"

"Did you hear what I said?"

She nodded, then remembered Rei couldn't see her. "Bully for you," she said dryly.

Reilly's laugh made her scowl even more.

"What's so funny?"

"You are," Rei said. "I should have known better than to spring that on you first thing in the morning—well, morning your time. For me it feels like it should be five in the afternoon.''

''That's because you get up at four in the morning.''

Mallory realized that it wasn't so much the morning that was bothering her, but all the tequila she'd drunk with Coco last night. Or earlier that morning, that is.

''Anyway, Layla and I are talking about having a double wedding.''

Yep, there was such a thing as too much good news. ''Oh, great.'' She rubbed the skin between her brows wondering if the wrinkle she felt was old or new. ''This blessed event is going to happen today, is it?''

''What? Oh, God, no!''

''Good, then let me call you back.''

Mallory pressed disconnect then felt around blindly to put the cell back on her nightstand. She felt like her mouth was stuffed with steel wool and her eyelids were glued together.

She really should get up. Call Reilly back and apologize for being so rude. But she couldn't seem to summon the energy to swing her legs over the bed much less make a dash for the bathroom.

She slapped the sheet down and looked around her bedroom. For a moment, she almost didn't recognize it. Oh, yeah. She'd cleaned up the place last night.

She somehow managed to get her feet under her and shuffle to the bathroom and see to business. Then she headed to the kitchen where she put on some coffee to brew with real filters. The only thing she allowed herself to buy out of the money her friends had given her. (The way she saw it, if she were to function as a filmmaker, caffeine was a must.) While the coffeemaker spit and hissed, she headed into the dining room and stared at the neat stack of folders and files she'd put in order. Only they weren't in the order she remembered putting them.

She scratched her head and leafed through the top few files. Then her cell phone rang from the bedroom just as someone knocked at her door. She opened the door first, mindless that all she had on was a T-shirt and underpants, held up a finger to Candy, then stalked toward the bedroom. She picked up the phone.

"Is it an emergency?" she asked.

Hesitation, then Layla said, "No. I was just calling to see if you heard Reilly's news."

"Yes. I'll call you back."

She disconnected then walked back into the living room to find Candy standing inside the door, her pink silk robe held closed with one hand.

"Is Coco here?" she asked.

Mallory blinked several times. "Close the door. That light is enough to blind a body."

Candy did.

"Now repeat your question."

But she didn't stand to wait. Instead she headed back into the kitchen and poured herself a cup of coffee then laced it with sugar and cream. She took an experimental sip then sighed. Heaven.

"I guess Coco isn't here," Candy said, looking around. "Hey, you cleaned. The place looks great."

"Thanks," Mallory managed, taking another sip of coffee. "Why would Coco be here?"

Candy shrugged. "I don't know. When I woke up this morning she wasn't in the apartment. And neither was her luggage."

Mallory lifted her brows.

"I thought maybe she'd moved in with you for a while. We, um, kind of had a fight last night."

"She didn't mention that." She shook her head. "She came here with a bottle of tequila but she left at around four or five. I thought she was going back to your place."

Candy sighed and shook her head. "Are you going to offer me some of that?"

Mallory looked between her and her coffee cup then shook her head. "I thought you didn't do coffee. Something about skin or something. Anyway, if you'd let me have the Sara Lee the other day, I would think about it. But since you didn't…"

Candy rolled her eyes then headed toward the door in her pink mules. "Your loss. I have triple chocolate cake thawing in the fridge now. From Sugar 'n' Spice.''

Mallory ran into the kitchen to fill a cup then hurried after Candy. Chocolate, chocolate, chocolate...

Someone stepped to block her path.

Jack.

Forget chocolate. One look at Jack and her body was pumping enough adrenaline to fuel a girls' soccer team.

"Reilly told me you were back from Omaha,'' he said. "And that you were up.''

She nodded, watching as Candy closed her door across the courtyard, the temptation of chocolate still lingering. She could always take Jack with her. "I'm back. And I'm up. Let's go.''

Jack caught her across the shoulders. "Whoa. Where do you think you're going dressed like that?''

"Chocolate,'' she said simply and pointed to Candy's apartment.

He held up a bag. "Sticky buns.''

"Oh, oh, oh, oh!'' Mallory snatched the bag from his hand, pulled him inside, then slammed the door. "Have I told you how much I love you?''

Silence.

Mallory had half a bun in her mouth when she realized what she'd said. Nothing like mucking up a perfectly good moment with a stupid comment like that.

It was way too early in the morning to delve into a complicated issue like life, love and Jack. Especially since so much of it involved unresolved problems with her mother and all she had come to believe about who she was and who she wanted to be. It was probably a pretty good idea to work through all that before she even thought about love and Jack.

She made a face. What was she talking about? He probably hadn't even caught the slip.

She slowly turned to look at him, finding his expression handsomely stunned.

Oops. He *had* caught it.

Mallory tried to swallow the unchewed food as she waved her bun-filled hand. ''I love that you brought me sticky buns, I mean,'' she said.

Unfortunately, given the change of his expression, she wasn't sure her correction was all that much better.

''Uh-huh,'' JACK SAID quietly.

He'd known what she'd meant. But her explanation had completely ruined that instant of ''what if.'' What if it were true and Mallory admitted to it?

What if they stopped running around the mulberry bush and recognized they were meant to be together?

The last one caught even him off guard. But as he thought about it, he knew it was true. He wanted Mallory in his life, in his bed, every morning of every day. He wanted to wake up with his arousal pressed against her bare backside and his fingers cupping one of her breasts. He wanted to hear her grumbling until after she had her second cup of coffee. Wanted to anticipate which offensive T-shirt she would wear. Wanted to anticipate the moment when he'd be able to peel off that T-shirt and see what kind of naughty underwear she had on underneath.

Damn it, he wanted her.

And she wasn't going to let him have her.

He scratched the nape of his neck then smoothed his hair back down. Did that even make any sense?

She'd turned away from him as she devoured the sticky bun, knocked back coffee and went through files on her dining room table. The purple T-shirt she wore barely covered her backside, revealing the sweet curve of her bottom cheeks as she moved. His mouth watered, and his reaction had nothing to do with sticky buns, but with Mallory's buns.

The problem was that sex had stopped being enough a while ago.

Not a good position for him to be in.

On some subconscious level he had yet to understand completely, he suspected that was the entire reason he'd come up with his lamebrained ultimatum in the first place. He'd known he wanted something more with Mallory than just telling Layla and Reilly about their relationship. He wanted more of a relationship. But if he kept having just sex with her they'd never advance beyond that stage.

He grimaced. Wasn't it the woman who usually wanted something more? Who started talking wedding rings and nurseries and minivans? He found no amusement in the role reversal whatsoever.

"You've been doing some housekeeping," he remarked, looking over the unfamiliar apartment.

Mallory shrugged, her back still to him, the action causing the hem of her T-shirt to ride up even more.

Jack was filled with the urgent desire to press her hot little backside to his hard frontside.

"I can't be sure, but I think I'm missing some things," Mallory said quietly.

Jack blinked. "Like what?"

She gestured with a half-eaten sticky bun. "I don't know. The information I just picked up in Omaha for starters." She looked toward her bag, which rested against the wall near the door. "Maybe I'm mistaken. Maybe I haven't taken it out yet."

Mallory might be a lot of things—sexy as hell taking the top spot—but forgetful she was not. If she thought she'd put papers somewhere, then you could bet the mortgage that she had.

Jack stepped to the table next to her, eliminating the delectable view of her bottom. Which was just as well because he wasn't going to do anything, anyway. No. What he needed to do was figure out a way to get through to Mallory.

He picked up her coffee cup from the table and took a sip despite the sugary sweetness.

"Oh my God," she whispered, an edge of panic to the words.

Where Mallory's movements had been slow and methodical moments before, now they were fast and jerky. Jack had little choice but to take the sticky bun she thrust at him as she freed that hand to join in the search.

She stalked across the room, snatched up her backpack then dumped the contents all over the floor, dropping to her knees to go through them. So much for the clean place, Jack thought as he shrugged and finished off the bun.

Long minutes later Mallory completely stilled, her eyes wide as she stared off into space. "The check's gone."

Jack's chewing slowed, then stopped altogether. "What?"

Her eyes slowly shifted until she focused on him. "The check, the check! I can't find it."

She pushed to her feet to go through the items on the table again.

Jack narrowed his eyes. "Define gone."

She didn't say anything as her movements became frantic.

"Gone as in you spent it all? Gone as in you haven't cashed it yet? Gone as in you may have misplaced it?"

She stared at him. "Gone as in…gone."

She turned around, then around again, taking in the apartment and apparently trying to figure out where she might have put it.

"I cashed the check right after you brought me home the day before last. But I didn't take it all out in cash. Instead I took enough to cover Harris's salary, pay for the tickets to Omaha, and some overhead and editing expenses, then I had the bank issue me a cashier's check for the rest." She looked at him again. "I was going to give it back to you guys, you know, when I got the backing I needed. Speaking of which, what time is it?"

She grabbed Jack's arm and twisted it so she could read his watch.

"Oh God, oh God, oh God. I've got a half hour to get ready and get down to the James Foundation."

Jack was familiar with the James Foundation. Set up much as the Daniels Foundation his parents had wanted him to head up, it was a charitable organization created to help the filthy rich feel they weren't completely selfish. They awarded grants for higher education, for documentaries of note, funded research projects and helped the community at large by funding after-school activities for inner-city children and the like.

He watched Mallory rush for her bedroom, then stopped. "Drive me there?"

"Of course," Jack answered, although he still had countless questions he personally wanted answered.

First and foremost was why she wouldn't admit she loved him.

Coco HAD TAKEN THE CHECK; she must have.

Mallory sat outside the ornate meeting room of the James Foundation. She'd just spent the last two hours pitching her Red Gardenia documentary to two uptight men and one woman, none of whom had dropped their poker faces for a second to let her know how her presentation was going.

She'd worn a plain white, saying-free T-shirt, navy-blue blazer and slacks for the occasion. The polyester blend of the jacket made her arms itch and every couple of minutes she had to force herself not to scratch.

But why would Coco steal from her?

"Maybe because she needed the money, moron," she whispered under her breath.

Another guy sat in the waiting area with her and looked at her strangely. She smiled at him, stared at the closed meeting room door, then craned her neck to see outside where Jack, smoking a cigarette, leaned against his old Chevy.

She caught herself smiling, if only briefly. What that guy did for her. How many times had he waited patiently for her to see to some business or another—from shooting a background sequence to interviewing subjects—since her car had broken down? Broken down? Died was the more applicable word.

Still Jack had never complained once. She'd assumed it was because he had nothing better to do with his time. Now she was coming to realize that his being available for her was because he put her before everything else.

Her heart gave a painful squeeze as she thought about all the accusations she'd lobbed his way over the past week.

"Are you here looking for a grant?" she asked the guy who sat across from her.

"Pardon me?" He looked at her, as though shocked that she'd spoken.

"A grant? Are you here to try to land one?"

He shook his head. "No. I'm here to interview for a position that would put me in charge of granting them."

"Ahhh," Mallory said, wondering if she should be extra nice to him, you know, in case he got the job and ended up on the other side of that table the next time she pitched to the foundation.

She squinted at him. Just how, exactly, did one go about getting one of those jobs, anyway?

Ten to one he was related to someone who sat on the board.

She cleared her throat to keep herself from saying anything. Implying nepotism would definitely not endear him to her, no matter how true it might be.

She caught herself scratching again and fisted her hand and shoved it down between her thigh and the arm of the uncomfortable chair. They probably designed these places with the ultimate in discomfort in mind. To make the poor suckers like her suffer even more.

The door to the meeting room opened and Mallory leapt to her feet. Only it wasn't her the woman was after. Rather she waved in the other guy.

"Good luck!" Mallory called after him.

The moment the door closed again, she collapsed against the chair back and sighed. Yeah, right. Like luck had anything to do with his being there. More likely luck of birth was the only luck someone like him needed.

"Ms. Woodruff?"

The voice came from over her left shoulder. She shot up from the chair again to find a man she hadn't seen before addressing her. She fought against a frown and smiled instead. If the grant was given a thumbs-up, the panel would share the news themselves. When it was being denied, some lackey like this guy was the one who passed on the bad news.

She felt the cloud that had been following her around all morning open up and drench her.

If she feared the cloud had been trailing her for the entire five years she'd been in L.A…well, she wasn't quite up to admitting that yet.

12

ACID POOLED IN Jack's stomach as he sat across from Mallory on her living floor going through the pile of files she'd had stacked on the dining room table. Outside, the sun was already setting. From one of the other apartments came the sound of Christmas carols. The cheerful songs sounded strange against the serious atmosphere of Mallory's place. It seemed impossible to believe the holiday was less than a week away. Time seemed not to exist when he was with Mallory, but right this minute more than ever. Because Jack had the sinking sensation that something was changing. And it wasn't for the better.

They hadn't found the check. But they had found partial research information Mallory had done in Omaha, although the main file was missing. He fingered a photograph he guessed was of Jenny Fuller before she'd become The Red Gardenia. It was of a young man and woman, apparently at their senior prom. He recognized the woman as The Red Gardenia, but the man was unfamiliar—he squinted at the shot—or maybe not. There was something about him that made the back of Jack's neck itch.

"They're not here." Mallory stared at the wall over his shoulder.

They'd established that fact a few hours before after they'd returned from her grant interview. But they'd searched through her things another dozen times just to be sure and Mallory had disappeared for a while to her neighbor Candy's from where Coco Cabana had also disappeared, conveniently at the same time as the check and the file.

"I can't believe she'd take the file," Mallory whispered, the color drained from her face. "Okay, I can see her taking the check, but why take the file?"

Jack began reorganizing the mess littering the floor between them. "You don't even know her, Mallory."

She didn't say anything for a long moment, then she shifted her eyes to look at him and gestured with her hands. "I never said I did. But I never left her alone in my place, either, which means she had to have broken in to get at the stuff." She shook her head. "I don't get it."

Jack had ordered pizza but Mallory had barely touched a piece of pepperoni much less an entire slice and he knew she hadn't had anything to eat since the sticky buns that morning.

She was preoccupied. More than that, she was as somber as he'd ever seen her.

He watched as she rested her elbows on her knees then dropped her head into her hands. "That's it. It's over."

Jack blinked. Over? As in...them? "What?"

She stayed like that, silent, for long minutes, then looked up at him. But her smile looked a little false. Her eyes overly bright and empty. "Oh, well. You live and you learn, right?"

All Jack knew was a tremendous relief that she hadn't been talking about them.

"Where's that pizza?" she said, getting up from the floor and moving toward the dining room table.

Then she appeared to change her mind and did an about-face, staring at him instead. Given the predatory expression she wore, he guessed he now knew what a pizza put in front of Mallory might feel like.

Before Jack could blink she was straddling his hips and pushing him to the floor, tearing at his shirt and launching an attack on his mouth.

"Whoa," he said, chuckling as he held her back slightly. "Where did that come from?"

"I'm horny and you're available." She kissed either side of his mouth then his lips full on. "Do you need anything more than that?"

Yes, he wanted to say, he *did* need more.

But her surprise attack was leaving him incapable

of explaining what exactly it was that he needed from her beyond to touch her, to have her touch him, and to feel her all over.

She peeled her T-shirt over her head then started on the button of the jeans she'd changed into when they'd returned from the foundation earlier. Jack's mouth watered as she revealed inch after precious inch of her sweet flesh. Mallory didn't work out so she wasn't toned. She was one-hundred-percent soft, rounded female. And he wanted her…loved her so much it hurt.

"You're not getting undressed," she said, climbing off him to take off her jeans.

He shook his head. "I'm enjoying watching you undress."

When she'd stripped down to her panties and bra she started on him. Jack sat back and watched her breasts sway as she made history of first his shirt, then his shoes, socks and jeans. His erection pressed against the front of his boxers. Well, at least for a millisecond before she took his underwear off as well.

He swallowed hard. Being with Mallory had always been like being in the eye of a hurricane. Move a little to the left or the right and you were caught up in the worst of the storm. But now…now she seemed even more forceful, more determined. And Jack could do little more than watch as she took a condom from his pocket, sheathed him, then straddled him again with clear intent.

He held her aloft for a few precious seconds. "You asked me recently why I started drinking," he said quietly.

Her movements ceased, the only sound that of her ragged breathing. She didn't say anything from where her cheek rested against his, but he could imagine her expression to be open-eyed, expectant.

Jack smoothed his hands down her silky back. "I didn't answer you then. The truth is, I couldn't answer you. And I probably shouldn't be saying anything now..." But he had to. He sensed something about her tonight that he didn't quite like. That he wanted to change. "Let's just say that I'm still a little close to the subject."

He listened to her swallow hard. "But you stopped drinking a long time ago." She pulled back slightly to stare into his face. "Didn't you?"

He nodded. "Yes. Yes, I did. But what I feel for you..." He searched her beautiful face, finding warmth there. "What I feel for you is much like what I felt when I started drinking. Exhilarated. Free. Connected." He rubbed his thumbs over her cheeks. "The only problem was that, with booze, free and connected were illusions. Because when you rely on alcohol, well, you're neither free nor connected."

And when he relied on her while she was still

apparently intent on keeping him at arm's length…
well, that really wasn't any different, was it?

"Shh," she said, kissing his cheek then his
mouth. "We don't have to talk about this now."

He wanted to say that he wanted to talk about
this now. Needed to discuss it. But Mallory lowered
her slick flesh over his rigid shaft, and he could do
little more than close his eyes, reveling in the feel
of her surrounding him. Her scent, her touch. Give
himself over to that illusion of freedom and con-
nectedness.

He lifted up to lean on his hands and heard her
moan in response as he sat up. He curved her legs
behind his back then supported the weight of her
lush bottom with his hands. Then he merely was.
He didn't move. Didn't breathe. He only focused
on the sensations rushing through him. The red-hot
desire. The metallic feel in the pit of his stomach.
His need for her expanding to cover so many different levels that he couldn't think beyond right
here, right now.

She rested her forehead against his chin and took
a deep shuddering breath, apparently feeling the
weightiness of the moment as much as he was.

Jack slowly grasped her hips, tilting them forward so that her pubis rested directly against his,
his length filling her. The moment he'd met Mallory
three years ago, his own personal debate between

sex and making love had reached its conclusion. While he hadn't known it at the time—he'd only known an intense want of her physically—the second he'd looked into her eyes he'd known he'd met that one person who was meant for him. Who clicked with him. Who was the silhouette to his shadow. Their relationship had never been about just sex, no matter how many different ways Mallory tried to argue the point. And the key, itself, lay in the sex. They never tired of each other. Never felt the need to move onto another lover. They could make love ten times a day and it still wouldn't be enough.

No, it had never been just about the sex. Rather the answer to their true feelings for each other lay in the sex itself. It was the only time they laid themselves bare to the other. The only time that they pushed aside all the excuses, the lies—both to themselves and each other—and allowed their souls free reign over their bodies. Allowed their hearts to open wide and accept the other fully and unconditionally.

Mallory freed one of her hands from behind his back and rested it against his upper thigh, then leveraged herself against him. With slow, easy rolls of her pelvis she slid down then back up again, each stroke chasing the air from her exquisite body. Jack stared deep into her light brown eyes. He saw no hesitation, no fear, only sheer emotion. Emotion for him.

He pulled her down fast and he watched as her eyelids fluttered closed to cover her eyes and her lips parted on a low moan. Had he ever seen someone so beautiful? His gaze traveled down the solid column of her neck, the delicate curve of her collarbone, the soft swell of her breasts. The heat of their lovemaking manifested itself in a rosy glow on her skin, a glow only enhanced by the warm sheen of perspiration.

Jack released his hold on her hips and slid his hands around to her back, following her spine up to the clasp on her bra. He easily undid it and watched as the lacy material popped from her breasts and slid down her arms. He lowered his mouth to take one hardened peak into his mouth and felt his erection quiver deep inside of her. Mallory worked her fingers through his hair, drawing him even closer, her heart beating an erratic rhythm beneath the wall of her chest.

Sweet Jesus, this woman was going to be the end of him. The things she did to him without even trying. A simple blink of her eyes. A bite of her sharp wit. A wiggle of her bottom. Strange how little it took to turn him into a blathering idiot ready to drop to his knees and respond to her every little whim.

Of course, she didn't have a clue how he felt. Oh, she knew she could manipulate him into doing what she wanted. His taxiing her around was one

example of that. What she didn't know was that
he'd gladly drive her around for the rest of his life
and never want for anything more.

Anything but her.

And while he was currently as connected to Mallory as two people could be, he knew he was ignoring that acid in his stomach that was telling him
that not only didn't he have her, but that he would
never have her. Not fully. Not in the way he wanted
most.

Mallory braced her hands against his shoulders
and lifted herself up then sank back down on his
throbbing erection with slick, mind-blowing strokes.
Jack's internal dialogue ceased as pure sensation
took over. His mind stopped dictating his desires
and his body stepped in, accelerating the rate of his
heartbeat, stealing his breath, and unleashing a familiar chaos in his groin that built and built and
built.

Mallory moaned, her breasts skimming against
his chest as she reached for her own climax and
caught it. As her soft, wet muscles convulsed
around him, he couldn't help but give himself over
to his own orgasm.

As the spasms subsided, Jack held her tight
against his chest, almost afraid to let go. He
couldn't quite explain why he sensed that he might
lose her if he did, but he couldn't get rid of the
feeling either.

She slowly kissed his shoulder, her breathing ragged, her hands sliding down his sweat-covered back.

"Jack…I'm going home."

KANSAS CITY.

Home.

Now there was a word.

Mallory nipped at the salty skin of Jack's shoulder, then rubbed her cheek against the toned flesh, a pain so gigantic expanding in her chest that she was surprised it didn't crack right through her rib cage.

She hadn't known that was how she would feel when she'd said the words. But she would never have guessed her reaction to be so acute.

Jack tried to pull her back so he could look into her face. She counteracted by clinging to him more tightly.

She couldn't look at him just yet. She needed to let her own decision sink in before she could be anywhere near ready to deal with his reaction to it.

She'd given herself five years to make it in L.A. And that five years had reached its conclusion. It was over. She didn't have what it took. It was as simple as that. For nearly two thousand days she'd scraped to make the rent, to feed herself, to make the kind of films she'd always dreamed of making. And with the disappearance of her friends' investment in her...well, she'd proven that she wasn't even a good friend.

"Mall..." Jack said in a low voice. "Talk to me. What did you mean just then? Define home?"

"Kansas," she whispered.

She felt Jack stiffen under her, but not in the way she might have liked at that moment.

"I just...can't do this anymore."

She finally gave in to his attempt to pull her back so he could look at her. Only she couldn't bring herself to look into his eyes.

"What?" The one word came out in a hushed whoosh.

Mallory nodded. "I don't have what it takes, Jack. I've tried...and I've failed. It's time for me to admit that now. To accept that I'm no filmmaker. I'm just an overly ambitious, simple girl from Kansas City."

His fingers tightened on her arms. "You are not simple."

That made her want to smile and she finally lifted her gaze to him. "Well, it looks like I've got you fooled, anyway." She swallowed hard, the emotion pushing from her chest and moving up her throat. "But I can't go on fooling myself anymore, Jack. I...I can't even pay my rent for God's sake. I'm a call to the sheriff's office away from being evicted. I used the cut-out foot of my nylons for a coffee filter the other day. Rock bottom. That's where I've hit.''

"But your documentaries."

She stared at a mole on his chest just above his left nipple. How she loved to nibble at the tiny mole. It hurt to think she wouldn't be able to do that anymore. And it hurt even more to think that someday someone else would be doing what she so loved to do. "My documentaries have gone nowhere."

She could tell he was restraining himself from shaking her. "You've won awards."

"And I can't get a grant or funding to save my life."

"You've got a great eye."

"Which means absolutely zip if no one wants to see my work."

He shifted her so that they were no longer connected. "You can't just give up, Mallory. That's not like you. You always have plans."

She was surprised at the sob that bubbled up her throat. "Yes, well, I'm fresh out just now. I gave myself five years to become a successful filmmaker and it didn't happen. Maybe I've just been lying to myself. Maybe who I am in this one moment is more me than either of us knew about."

He stared at her for long, silent moments. "No," he said, shaking his head. "I won't let you give up."

Mallory hated to do it, hated to end things so abruptly between them, but she got up from his lap and slowly began redressing. "You don't have any say in the matter, Jack."

"Try me."

She looked over her shoulder to find him still sitting in the same spot, gloriously naked, staring at her in clear challenge. "What do you propose to do? Tie me up in your closet?"

"I'll give you the money Coco stole."

A sadness so powerful, so acute, washed over Mallory as she finished redressing, that she nearly dropped to her knees with the enormity of it. "You just don't get it, do you? I can't take money from you or Layla or Reilly. I should never have taken what I did."

"Then move in with me."

Her breath froze in her lungs. Oh, no fair. She turned away and began gathering up the files that such a short time ago meant the world to her but now represented nothing but failure.

"I can't," she said.

She didn't realize Jack had gotten up to stand behind her until he swung her around to face him. "Why?"

Mallory clutched the files to her chest. "Because it's not something I do, that's why." She took a deep breath. "I don't live off of people like my mother does. I don't feed off of them. I don't size up the men and women I meet in terms of dollar signs and ease of manipulation.''

''Mallory, we're your friends.'' His voice dropped and his eyes darkened. ''I'm your friend.''

She smiled sadly. ''And that's why I can't take advantage of you.''

He gripped her so tightly she gasped and dropped the files. ''You wouldn't be taking advantage of anybody, Mall. Layla, Reilly and me? We're here for you. Through thick and thin. So you were robbed. It could happen to any one of us. So we find a way to deal with it. We work it out—together—and find a way around it.''

She slowly shook her head. ''Don't make this harder than it already is, Jack. I...I don't think I can stand it.''

''And me?'' he asked, his voice barely above a whisper. ''What do you think this is doing to me?''

It was killing him. She could see it in his deepset expression. The tortured shadow in his eyes.

''I...I can't think about that,'' she whispered. ''Not now. I've...''

She had to stop talking, had to try to gather her wits about her. The pain in her chest was spreading, grabbing a hold of her lungs, making it impossible to breathe.

She hiccupped as she looked into Jack's eyes. ''I've never lied to you, Jack. I've never told you I was staying forever. I never said anything about a future.'' She rubbed the heel of her hand over her nose, wondering where the smart-ass Mallory had gone off to and just where she might find her again.

Then again, the smart-ass Mallory had been the one to get her into so much trouble. She'd been so busy making the plans that Jack had referred to that she hadn't seen what else was happening. She'd misled herself into believing that she could be somebody she was not. Could never be. Made herself think that a girl from Kansas could be a filmmaker. Deluded herself into thinking that she belonged in this magical place. Fooled herself into thinking that she was different, deeper than the filmmakers she'd dubbed as shallow and uninspired.

Instead she was afraid that she was the one who was shallow and uninspired. That the labels she'd stuck on others were stuck all over her instead.

But smart-ass Mallory had made her ignore that. Had filled her with false ambition and driven her to a dead end in the road she'd thought would roll on forever.

She blinked, realizing Jack was pulling on his jeans. He snapped upright and started shaking his head. ''I'm not going to make this easy for you, Mallory. I'm not going to let you leave like this.''

A small spark ignited in her veins. ''Don't do this, Jack. I don't want to hurt you any more than I already will. But if you try to force the issue, I'll rip your heart out and put it through the shredder.''

She picked up the files at her feet again then walked into the kitchen and dumped them into the trash container. He followed but before he could say anything she turned back to him.

"Damn you! Damn you all to hell, Jack! I told you to keep this…casual. Not to push me…push us. But no, you wouldn't listen. You wanted to tell Layla and Reilly. You wanted to blow up what we shared into an entire relationship."

A muscle in his jaw ticked. "I didn't do anything. It happened all by itself. And if you'd stop listening to all the crap you're trying to sell me on, maybe you'd see it, too."

He was right, of course. She had known for a long time now that what she and Jack shared was more than sex. Had known it and ignored it. What kind of person went into a relationship not knowing who they were and what they were capable of?

It didn't take her long to think of just that kind of person. Her mother.

And look what had happened to her.

She was on her twentieth victim. *Oh, excuse me, boyfriend.* And just last week she had told Mallory things looked promising, that he would become husband number seven.

And if there was one thing in this world that Mallory knew she wasn't, it was her mother.

"How long have you had this five-year rule?" Jack asked.

Mallory blinked, surprised by the question. "Since the day I first set foot in L.A."

"And you never said anything. Not to me. Not to Layla. Not to Reilly."

"No." Because to do so would have been to admit that she saw failure as an option. And she hadn't been ready to acknowledge that. Until now. Until right this very minute.

"Come on, Jack," she whispered, desperately wishing she could wipe the pain from his face, from his heart. She rested her palm against his chest. "Do you really think it would have made a difference?"

His eyes narrowed and he caught her hand when she might have taken it away. "Yes," he said as simply as she'd said no. "It would have made a difference because I would never have allowed myself to fall in love with you."

13

A SHORT TIME LATER, Jack felt like he was moving through neck-deep seawater as he walked from his car to his apartment. His body seemed as shocked as his mind and heart.

Mallory was leaving him.

Not just him, but L.A.

He might have been able to stand it if she was leaving just him. But to imagine her not even being in the same state, much less the same city, did things to him that he couldn't begin to describe.

He opened the door to his apartment expecting to see Boomer lying in the foyer. He wasn't there. He always left lights on for the old dog, but he couldn't see him anywhere.

"B?" he called out.

Nothing.

Concern for his long-time pet piled on top of the jumble of other emotions that had been stirred up that night.

He flipped on the overhead light in the kitchen. Boomer's food was untouched. He went to the door to the small yard area, but he wasn't out there, either.

Five minutes later he'd searched everywhere but still no sign. Not in the living room, not in the bedroom. It appeared he had disappeared.

He flicked on the light in the bathroom. The sound of heavy breathing caught his attention. He stepped to the bathtub and pulled back the shower curtain. There Boomer lay on his side panting. If he was aware that Jack was standing over him, he didn't indicate.

Not normal. Definitely not normal. Boomer had always avoided the bathtub like the plague. That he was lying in there now nearly unconscious was indicative of a very serious problem.

"Hang in there, buddy. Hang in there. Everything's going to be okay."

Jack scooped up the old, ailing dog and rushed for the door, hoping that he was right, that everything would be okay. But he had the sick sensation that nothing in his life was going to be okay again.

THE FOLLOWING EVENING Mallory stood in her tiny kitchen, taping up the last of the boxes she was giving to Candy.

Nearly everything was packed. It depressed her to think that she'd lived there for what seemed like a lifetime, yet she could fit all her belongings into three medium-size boxes. Of course, she'd already given a lot of her stuff to Candy, who would probably pass it on to one of her adoptees. Her latest roommate was a guy named Jeremy who had been living on the streets since coming in by bus from Milwaukee some ten months before. Maybe he'd be able to use her old pots and pans when he eventually got his own place. The only thing Mallory was taking from the kitchen was her coffeemaker. She could live without everything else, but not her coffeemaker.

Of course, she refused to think about how she was going to live without Layla and Reilly.

And Jack.

Her breath hitched in her throat. God, she hadn't even known this kind of emotional pain could manifest itself in such a physical manner. Sometimes it hurt just to breathe. Last night as she'd lain awake staring at the ceiling, she'd tried to convince herself that it was the death of her dream, her career ambitions, that had made her feel like her life had been turned upside down.

But every time she closed her eyes she saw Jack's stunned face. His words rang in her ears.

He loved her.

Of course, she'd known that. Had never really acknowledged it, even to herself, but she had known it. But the words coming on the heels of her own news had cut her straight to the bone.

He loved her.

And she was leaving.

But she *had* to leave. Why couldn't anybody understand that?

There was a brief knock on her door. She glanced toward it then hoisted the box to give it to Candy.

"This is the last of them," she said, balancing the box and opening the door.

Only it wasn't Candy standing on her doorstep. Rather it was Layla and Reilly.

She didn't realize she was looking for Jack until she concluded he wasn't with them.

"Expecting someone else?" Layla asked, her arms crossed in that way that told Mallory she was loaded for bear.

Mallory swallowed hard and put the box down by the door. "Yes, as a matter of fact, I was. Candy."

"Mmm-hmm," Reilly said, following Layla inside and closing the door.

Mallory readjusted the position of the box she'd just put down, reluctant to turn toward her friends.

"You might as well stop pretending that box needs your attention and face us," Reilly said.

Mallory stood up and stiffened, not sure she was up for this just then. Not sure she would ever be up for it.

"Surely you didn't think it was going to be that easy," Layla said, not having moved from her spot near the door. "A five-minute phone call telling me you're leaving for Kansas on the first bus out in the morning. For good.''

''What did you honestly expect us to do? Wish you happy trails and disappear into the woodwork?'' Reilly asked.

''It, um, would have helped,'' Mallory said dryly.

Reilly laughed and Mallory just now realized her friend held something in her hand. Reilly took out a bottle of premixed margaritas along with three plastic cups and set them out on the empty dining room table that Candy would be picking up in the morning along with the rest of her furniture. The plan being that Candy would get there before the super would.

She stood stock still, watching as Layla and Reilly prepared what must have been intended as a going away party of sorts. A corn chip bag was opened, a jar of salsa, a takeout box of burritos from her favorite Mexican restaurant up the street and, a must, a tray of sticky buns.

Mallory's throat grew tight as she watched the two women chatter while they set out the buffet then positioned the chairs around the table. These two women had grown so very dear to her. No matter what she said to them, how cutting her remarks could be—past comments had nearly caused Reilly and Ben to break up permanently, for God's sake!— they loved her anyway.

Could she really say that about another woman?

Oh, sure, she supposed her mother loved her. A mother was required to love her child, wasn't she? At least to some degree. But Mallory had never been close to her, never came to understand her, and she was sure the same applied to her mother, who was puzzled why Mallory hadn't married at eighteen, much less was still single at twenty-four.

But Layla and Reilly...

Layla and Reilly felt like home. More than family, really, although not even Mallory could say what that classification would be. She just knew that she loved them.

Yes, she loved them.

When they hurt, she hurt.

When they were happy, she was happy for them.

Well, okay, most of the time she was happy for them.

At any rate, it was that much more painful to leave knowing that she wouldn't be five minutes away from them anymore. That she couldn't just pop into Sugar 'n' Spice and raid the display case while they all gossiped about the customers or discussed their love lives or were just plain catty.

Four plastic cups of margaritas later, Mallory was surprised that rather than dulling her pain, the alcohol merely seemed to amplify it.

"...then Mall comes in, walks up to their table and says, 'So how's it feel to know you were both doing the same guy?'" Reilly slapped her hand over her heart and howled with laughter. "I swear, I thought I was going to die on the spot."

Mallory fought to focus on what her friend was saying. Oh, yeah. She was talking about two women who had dropped into Sugar 'n' Spice on a regular basis. They ended up becoming friends, but then found out that the one's husband and the other's boyfriend were the same man.

She smiled to indicate she understood but couldn't summon the energy to respond further.

"Where's Jack?" she asked when a lull fell in the conversation.

It was a question she'd wanted to pose the moment she'd spotted them on her doorstep but hadn't dared ask until several margaritas had taken effect.

Layla shared a look with Reilly that made her heart sink in her chest.

"What?" she asked, sitting forward and nearly knocking her plastic glass over. "What is it? What's happened?"

"We didn't know if you'd heard or not, so we didn't want to saying anything…"

Mallory grasped Layla's arm, her heart racing a million miles a minute. "What is it? Has he been in an accident? I've told him about that damn car of his. He drives like a maniac…"

"Boomer's dying, Mall."

Her heart stopped beating altogether.

Boomer. His dog. His best friend outside the

three of them. A dog that had helped him get through the rough times when he'd stopped drinking.

A dog that he loved with all of his heart.

Reilly cleared her throat. "He took him to the vet last night. They've tried everything they could all day, but Boomer's old. First there was kidney failure, then...well, it seems everything is collapsing all at once. There's nothing they can do."

Mallory began to get up on shaky knees. "Which vet? Where? I've got to go to them."

Layla caught her arm, preventing her from moving from the table. "Mall, Jack asked us not to tell you."

She stared at her friend as if she'd just uttered gibberish. "What?"

Reilly nodded. "Layla's right. Jack specifically asked that we not say anything to you. He said he wanted to be alone with Boomer when he, you know, passed."

"Are you crazy?" Mall said. "He can't be left alone. That dog means the world to him!"

"So do you," Layla said plainly.

Mallory searched her friends' eyes. What were they trying to say?

"Jack says that he doesn't want Boomer to be the reason you put off going back to Kansas."

"I don't care what Jack said!" Mallory was

pretty sure she was yelling but she couldn't help herself.

She strode toward the door.

"How do you think you're going to get there?" Reilly asked.

"Cabs won't come to this part of town this late," Layla pointed out.

Mallory marched back to the table, grabbed Layla's purse, then pulled out her car keys.

"Whoa, whoa, whoa," Layla said, making a grab for her keys. "I'm not letting you drive in your condition."

Mallory held the keys out to her. "Then you drive. But I'm telling you right now, Layla, one way or another I will get to that vet's office."

Twenty minutes later they were sitting outside the vet's, but they were too late. Jack had left a half hour ago, the attendant had told them. Yes, Boomer had died quietly in his sleep, his owner at his side.

Mallory sat in the passenger's seat, the weight of everything that had accumulated during the past two days too much for her to handle.

She started crying, and couldn't seem to stop.

VERY EARLY THE NEXT morning Jack sat within reach of the vodka bottle, staring at it in naked challenge. He craved the liquid with a passion. Thirsted for it with a need that should have scared him, but didn't.

He reached out with open hand, then halted midway there. He closed his fingers into a fist then dropped the hand back down into his lap.

He'd never had a pet before Boomer. As a boy, he'd never been allowed one. Dogs were dirty animals that needed constant care and attention, his mother had said whenever he'd asked for a puppy—which was every Christmas until he was thirteen years old when he knew better than to make the request. She wasn't going to pay the servants to look after his pet. And forget what a puppy would do to the antique Persian rug in the foyer!

Jack closed his eyes and ran his hands over his face. The morning he'd found Boomer roaming, lost, in the park, he'd been sure he belonged to somebody. He'd been no more than three months old. Had on a red, spiked collar. And whined in a way that made his chest hurt. After he'd tried to locate his owner and came up empty handed, he'd scooped up the little pup and been rewarded with his first ever face licking.

He'd been wrapped around Boomer's little paw ever since.

Tonight he'd held that same paw and watched as Boomer ran away from him forever.

It wasn't fair. There should be a law somewhere that dictated that pets live at least as long as their owners. If someone had told him when he'd found Boomer on that fateful day ten years ago that he'd be sitting right where he was now, mourning him, he would have found someone else to take the pup posthaste.

He knew a moment of pause.

Then again, no.

He'd had ten years with the playful pup. And even when the hound had developed arthritis and hadn't been able to move the way he once could, Jack could tell with one look into his watery brown eyes that the pup still resided within.

He blew out a long breath and sat back in the chair, glancing toward Boomer's bed filled with all his toys. At somewhere around midnight he'd heard pounding on his door. Mallory. But he couldn't bring himself to answer it. He'd been sitting right where he was now, in a mock Mexican standoff with the vodka bottle. And he knew he couldn't handle her grief for Boomer on top of his own. Not when he knew she was leaving him, too.

He glanced at the clock on the end table to his right. 4 a.m. What time had Layla said Mallory's bus was leaving? Eleven?

Adrenaline coursed through his veins at the thought of rushing to that bus station and doing everything he could to stop her from boarding. His shoulders slumped. But the determination in Mallory's face when she'd said she was going home told him nothing short of throwing himself at her feet and grabbing her ankles would stop her. In fact, he suspected she'd kick his hands away and step right over him in order to do what she was setting out to.

It had been that same determination that had kept her in L.A. for five years.

It was that same single-mindedness that had drawn him toward her, made him envious of her...of the fact that she knew what she wanted out of life and had a plan to go out and get it.

Where had that ambition gone?

It had disappeared along with the cashier's check Coco had made off with.

Jack's brain emptied out as he stared at the bottle again.

Check...Coco.

He absently rubbed the back of his neck, smoothing down the hairs that were standing on end there.

Then he pushed from the chair, snatched up the taunting vodka bottle and threw it into the trash, then made his way to Mallory's apartment as fast as he could.

MALLORY LAY ON HER BACK in the middle of the living room floor, having tried the bed, the couch and even a dining room chair in her attempt to get some sleep. But nothing was working.

She was still fully clothed. Her mouth felt like it was lined with chalk and her mind stuffed with terry cloth. Yet her eyes were still wide open and her brain click-clicked, incapable of shutting down.

Boomer had died.

Jack had shut her out.

In six-and-a-half hours she would be on a bus back to Kansas—quite possibly the same one that had brought her to California.

Her heavy sigh filled the empty apartment then seemed to echo back at her. She wished for some sort of sign that what she was doing was right. That she was making the right decision by packing it all in and going back home. Then again, the fact that nothing was stopping her plans was probably the biggest sign she was going to get.

Even the phone calls she'd made to her mother to tell her the news yesterday hadn't helped.

"Oh, thank God!" her mother had said. "I was afraid you might never come to your senses."

Mallory caught herself scratching her arm as though having an allergic reaction to the memory. Of course, Lucinda's enthusiasm only made her think homelessness might be preferable.

After a couple of phone calls to Kansas City employment agencies, she'd even managed to land a job in advertising at the local television station. So instead of making documentaries, she would be putting together used car commercials.

She winced, then sighed again.

Hey, it was a constant income. She would be

making a fair deal more than she'd ever made out here. And she'd be back with the people she'd grown up with, living in a place she knew like the back of her hand. L.A. and its sprawling suburbs still mystified the hell out of her.

It was like she was going backward in time to take up where she'd left off. If only she was looking forward to the trip...

"You'll get used to it," she whispered to herself.

Ah, wise words to live by, those. "You'll get used to it." That's what she'd said five years ago when she'd first gotten off the bus from Kansas at eleven o'clock at night and found herself staring at a city so unfamiliar, so frighteningly huge and so packed full of possibilities.

And she *had* gotten used to it.

She just hadn't *succeeded*.

Not in her career. Not in love. Not in life, period.

She glanced toward the far wall where she had yet to take Jenny Fuller's picture down. Had The Red Gardenia harbored any doubts about where she was going? Had she thought about walking back to the bus station and going home? Or had her path been a little rosier than Mallory's?

She swallowed hard. What a stupid question. Of course it hadn't been rosier. Jenny Fuller, aka The Red Gardenia, was dead and her killer had never been caught.

Marilyn Monroe had said, "Hollywood's a place

where they'll pay you a thousand dollars for a kiss, and fifty cents for your soul. I know, because I turned down the first offer often enough and held out for the fifty cents.''

And look where she landed.

Mallory swept her bangs back from her face with her hand and stayed like that for a long time.

Countless scandal pieces had been done on The Red Gardenia, but no real character pieces had been made about Jenny and the thousands of other girls like her who had followed their dreams to California only to have those dreams crushed.

There was a sound outside her apartment.

Mallory turned her head against the low pile carpeting to look toward the door and then the window. One of her neighbors calling it a night? More than likely.

She smiled humorlessly to herself. At least Layla could be happy about that. No longer would Mallory be living in an apartment complex filled with ''drug dealers and prostitutes.'' No, in Kansas she'd be living next to Susie Effin' Homemaker.

Well, at least Susie wouldn't steal from her.

She caught herself scratching her arm again. She'd pay the money to her friends if it killed her. Oh, they hadn't asked for it. In fact, neither Layla nor Reilly had said anything to her about it at all except that they were sorry the loss of it meant she was going back to Kansas.

She supposed the one saving grace was that she wouldn't have to spend Christmas with her mother. Layla and Sam and Reilly and Ben were getting married in a double ceremony in Vegas on Christmas Day and Layla had already given Mallory a plane ticket from Kansas City to the event.

She shook her head. Christmas Day in Vegas. She would never have thought either Layla or Reilly capable of such unconventional behavior.

Of course, she would go. If only to see her friends again.

If only to see Jack again.

Her heart pounded so hard she could swear she heard it. Why hadn't he answered his door earlier? She'd still be there now, camped out outside his apartment, if Layla and Reilly hadn't forcibly taken her back to her apartment.

Another sound from outside.

She squinted toward the light filtering in through the crack in the curtains, the same way she had the other night.

The night she'd caught Coco sneaking around outside.

She jackknifed to a sitting position, trying to make out any silhouettes on the other side of the curtain. Could it be Coco again? Come back to see what else she could take?

Then it struck her. Coco might not have had drinking tequila in mind at all when she'd shown up the other night. Maybe she'd arrived with the intention of robbing Mallory.

She got up and stormed toward the door, channeling all her mixed-up emotions into one angry ball that sat in the bottom of her stomach like a chunk of lead. She reached for the door handle, but stopped short, picking up her one and only lamp first.

She swung the door open and brought the lamp down on the shadowy person standing on the other side.

The lamp thudded against something hard then broke in two pieces and shattered against the pavement.

The figure fell over.

Mallory inched closer.

It wasn't Coco.

"Jack!"

14

JACK FELT LIKE HE HADN'T thrown the vodka bottle away at all, but that he'd downed it all in one long gulp.

Only he wasn't at his apartment. He was sitting on his butt outside Mallory's place, with what looked like a broken lamp scattered on the sidewalk alongside him.

"Oh my God!" Mallory cried.

Jack tried to focus on where she crouched next to him, but the world was a little blurry right now.

"What are you doing here?" she asked, brushing the lamp pieces out of the way then kneeling to check his head. "Oh, Jesus. You've got a bump the size of a Yugo on the back of your head."

Jack lifted his hand and gingerly explored the area in question with a little guidance from Mall. He also felt something wet and sticky. Blood. He closed his eyes. He and blood didn't get along very well.

"Come on, let's get you inside," Mallory said, trying to heft him to his feet by his arm.

But Jack was incapable of movement just then.

He sat there, imagining a cartoon of birds and stars circling his head. Whoever had drawn that cartoon first had obviously been through the experience himself.

"Expecting somebody else?" he grumbled, removing her hands from where she was probing his head again.

"I thought it might be Coco."

Jack's mind seemed to clear all at once as he remembered his reason for coming over. And also the reason he'd been standing with his back to Mallory when she'd opened the door.

Of course, if he hadn't had his back to her, he would have taken a lamp to the face.

Not a pretty image, that one.

He'd stumbled back a few feet before finally falling on his ass. Mallory's door still stood wide open and he blinked at it, then at her.

"I have the uncanny feeling that Coco isn't who we both think she...he is," he said.

"Tell me about it," Mall said, somehow managing to get him to his feet. Never underestimate the strength of a midget, Jack thought. "She's a thief."

"No. She's more than that."

Mallory nearly tripped trying to support his weight. He smiled down at her, feeling a little goofy. Getting hit in the head probably did that to a person.

"Do you still have the information you got in Nebraska?"

"Nebraska? What does Nebraska have to do with Coco?"

Jack reached out to steady himself on the doorjamb before Mallory got a hernia. She stepped inside and helped him follow her in.

"Just get the file, Mall," he grumbled. He recalled that he'd had some hangovers in his time that felt this bad. A strong reminder of why it was he didn't drink now.

He closed the door after himself and a light went on.

But judging from Mallory's gasp, she wasn't the one who'd flicked the switch.

Jack looked across the room at a woman holding a gun.

"Coco!"

Mallory couldn't believe that just five minutes ago she'd been lying on her floor bemoaning the ugly state of her life. Since then she'd beamed Jack on the head with a lamp thinking he was Coco. Then she'd come inside her apartment to find Coco holding a gun on her.

The aging prostitute—if that's what she really was—stood near the kitchen, while Mallory stood in the middle of the living room, and Jack was leaning against the closed door for support.

Coco waved the gun at Jack. "Move away from the door, lover."

The anger Mallory had felt when she'd picked up the lamp reemerged…and then some.

"You've got some nerve showing your face here again, Coco," she said, crossing her arms over her chest. "What's the matter? The cashier's check wasn't enough for you? Did you come back for more?"

The prostitute smiled, a malicious red slash in her makeup-covered face. "Move," she said to Jack again.

He began to push from the door then wavered on his feet. Mallory rushed to help him to the couch. He sank into the cushions then put his hands to his head. Mallory moved toward the kitchen to get some ice only to come face-to-face with Coco.

She swallowed hard, never having been that close to a gun before, but still ticked at all that had happened. "Is it all right if I get him some ice?"

Coco stepped to block her passage.

Mallory gulped. "Come on, where am I gonna go? There aren't any windows in the kitchen, so there's no way out."

To her surprise and enormous relief, Coco moved.

Mallory crossed to the refrigerator, only she had nothing in which to put the ice. So she ripped open the box on the counter, found a clean dishrag, then piled ice in the middle of it. Her gaze caught on the garbage bin and the files from the Red Gardenia case overflowing from the top. The one marked Nebraska was on top. Slanting a glance at where Coco had her back to her, the prostitute's major concern apparently Jack, Mallory took the file out, tucked it under her arm, then walked into the other room and sat down next to Jack.

"Here," she said, gently pressing the ice pack against the back of his head. She hated that her hands were shaking.

He made a low hissing sound then accepted the ice from her, holding it to his wound himself.

That freed her to sit back and open the Nebraska file.

"What are you doing?" Coco asked, advancing a few steps, the shiny silver gun held out in front of her.

Mallory ignored her and looked at Jack. "Is this what you were talking about?" she asked him.

He nodded, then winced at the movement. "The picture."

Mallory leafed through the documents as best she could, considering she didn't seem to have much control over her trembling hands at the moment. There was a picture of Jenny Fuller when she was thirteen. Then again at high school graduation. At the prom—

"That one," Jack said.

Mallory picked up the shot then let the rest of the file slide to the floor.

Jenny was seventeen in the shot, just about to turn eighteen and head out to California to make her dream of becoming an actress a reality. At her side was a tall, gangly boy, not quite a man, but not really a boy, either.

"Look familiar?" Jack asked.

Mallory looked closer at the boy's face.

"What is that?" Coco asked, advancing then snatching the photo from Mallory's hand.

Mallory blinked up into Coco's face.

Oh…my…God.

So it had been the file Coco had been after all along, not the check. Mallory had been the foolish one to stick the check in the file.

Coco stared at the shot then dropped it to her side. She heaved a heavy sigh. "I knew you were too close. Now it appears you've arrived."

"You," Mallory said, mentally banging the palm of her hand against her forehead.

She'd been so close. The murderer right under her nose almost from the start. And she'd never put two-and-two together.

Of course, neither had the cops.

But right now that was little consolation considering she had a gun pointed at her head.

Why was it suddenly difficult to breathe?

"I asked your real name," Mallory said nodding

thoughtfully, "you told me it was Arthur Black. The same initials as Arnold Barr."

Coco smiled then stuck the photo into the waist of her slim light wool skirt. "Do you think I've evaded the police for twenty-five years by being stupid?"

Mallory briefly closed her eyes. Why hadn't she seen it?

"Why?" she asked, staring steadily at Coco, aka Arnold Barr, and hoping she wasn't pushing her luck. "Jenny Fuller was your girlfriend. Your soul mate, your mom said. Why would you kill her?"

Jack leaned against Mallory's side. "Because he was jealous of her."

"Shut up. Just shut the hell up," Coco said, looking dangerously close to pulling off a round right into Jack's handsome face.

The shaking in Mallory's hands spread to include the rest of her body, until she was pretty sure she resembled a divining rod directly above an underground lake.

"I killed Jenny because I wasn't enough for her. I was just someone to pass the time with until she could come to L.A. But I didn't figure that out until after she left."

Mallory watched as the aging prostitute began pacing back and forth across the floor. She felt better when she moved farther away, hated when she came closer. "So you followed her."

"Damn right I followed her." She snorted and waved the gun.

A shot rang out and stuffing arced out from the couch a few inches from Mallory's leg.

Coco looked shocked.

Mallory was sitting on Jack's lap holding onto him for dear life, not entirely sure there weren't any holes in her person.

When it was apparent the shot had been a mistake, Jack cleared his throat and put Mallory back down. Mallory wanted to object. "Well, we now know it's definitely loaded."

Mallory didn't think she'd be able to walk without her knees knocking together again. "Be careful where you point that damn thing," she whispered.

Coco was still staring at the firearm as she said, "Jenny never knew I was following her. I'd call her from across the street of her apartment and pretend I was calling from Omaha. I'd watch as she'd pick up the phone and feed me lies about how wonderful it was here and how much hope she had for the future."

"You were hoping she would fail and come back home to you," Mallory said.

"Of course I was! What else was there for me in Omaha without her? I'd built my entire future plans around her. Nothing made sense if she wasn't in the picture."

Her gaze was drawn to the poster of The Red

Gardenia on the wall. She walked across to it and stroked Jenny's cheek with the muzzle of the gun. "Then she got this gig and everywhere I looked there she was. The Red Gardenia. She didn't get paid crap for the job. But the exposure..."

Jack finished. "The exposure was enough to catapult her into fame."

Coco slowly let the gun drop to his side.

"How come she never spotted you?" Mallory asked.

Coco turned and smiled bitterly. "A guy at the homeless shelter turned me on to opportunities for transvestites. It was the perfect way to disguise myself. I could follow Jenny without her even knowing I was there."

"But she figured it out," Mallory said.

Coco looked down at the gun as if surprised to find it there. "She called me in Omaha one day and my mother told her I'd come to California. That same day she ran smack dab into me." She smiled sadly. "Makeup wasn't very good back then. But I don't think that would have made a difference. She had just talked to my mother and was probably looking for me." He shrugged.

"I take it she wasn't happy to see you."

Coco smirked. "Not wearing one of her favorite dresses, she wasn't." He turned away again. "I would sneak into her place while she was gone and borrow her things, then put them back again when

I was done so she never had a clue anything was missing. If she couldn't find something one day, she'd find it the next.''

"Why her feet?" Mallory suddenly asked, then shuddered.

She remembered reading that Jenny's feet had been cut off.

She wasn't much on shoes, but she valued her own feet and would prefer to keep them. Right now, however, the prospects for that weren't looking too good.

Coco stretched out one leg, staring at her own foot that looked about size twelve. "I always loved her feet. So small, so delicate.''

Jack sat up a little higher. "By then you discovered you liked being a woman, didn't you, Arnold?"

"Don't call me that!" she shrieked.

Mallory resisted the urge to slap her hand over Jack's mouth.

Coco cleared her throat. "My name is Coco. Coco Cabana.''

Mallory whispered. "No, he didn't want to be a woman. He wanted to be her.''

Before Mallory could blink, Jack was charging Coco/Arnold. Another shot rang out, nailing the couch on the other side of Mallory. She squealed and leapt from the cushions, picking up her other lamp then bringing it down on top of Coco's too-blond head.

Coco collapsed on top of Jack and they both fell to the floor.

Mallory stood, still holding the lamp, taking in the sight of Coco unconscious on top of Jack.

Jack stared at her. "Thanks a lot."

The lamp slipped out of Mallory's hand then broke on the floor. "Don't mention it," she thought she said, but couldn't be sure because she was two blinks away from fainting dead away.

SEVEN HOURS LATER, the departure time for Mallory's bus had come and gone, Layla and Reilly had shown up for the scheduled "see Mallory to the station" send-off. Jack stood off to the side of the bus station watching as Mallory turned in her ticket to exchange it for one for a bus leaving for Kansas in an hour.

It seemed unreal, somehow, watching what he was. His head still throbbed, Coco Cabana, aka Arnold Barr, was in jail and Mallory was still leaving.

"Are you sure you really want to do this?" Reilly was saying as Mallory checked her ticket then stuck it into the back pocket of her jeans.

Jack followed the movement of her hand, taking in her curvy backside for what would probably be the last time.

Well, the last time until Las Vegas.

Maybe he shouldn't go to Layla and Reilly's double wedding. They'd probably understand that it was hard enough for him to watch Mallory go once. To have to let her go twice…

Well, twice would probably send him diving right into the contents of a new vodka bottle.

He absently rubbed his chin as he stared at everyone but Mallory—until she was standing right in front of him, filling his vision, crowding his senses.

She gave him a sad half smile. "I'm sorry…"

He looked down and nodded.

"You know, about Boomer. And about…well, everything."

"Me, too," he said quietly.

Then she was wrapping those arms of hers around his neck and pressing her sweet little body against his. He knew a craving so deep that it was all he could do not to clamp her to him and carry her out of there and back to his apartment.

Instead, he lightly placed his hands on her hips and bent his head to her sweet-smelling neck.

Oh, hell, he was going to miss her.

Mallory pulled back away from him and cleared her throat, smiling awkwardly at where Layla and Reilly stood nearby, watching. "You, um, guys don't have to stay. I know you have other things you need to be doing."

Not me, Jack wanted to say.

But he didn't, because he knew the wisest thing

to do was to get out of there. Before he made an even bigger fool out of himself.

He nodded.

"Tina's got a class in an hour so I really should be getting back to the shop," Reilly said quietly and hugged Mallory tightly.

Layla followed suit. "I could stay with you if you want."

Mallory shook her head. "No. Don't. It will only make things harder."

She turned back to Jack.

They just stood there like that, staring at each other in the middle of the bustling bus station. Jack had no idea what to say, so he didn't say anything.

She gave him a little wave and began walking toward the bus.

Jack felt as though Freddy Krueger of *A Nightmare On Elm Street* fame had just paid him a visit and dragged his knives right down the middle of Jack's chest. He couldn't seem to draw a breath. His legs felt like they might collapse out from underneath him at any moment. And his heart beat so hard against his rib cage it sounded like knocking.

Mallory climbed up the two stairs, an older man following after her.

Then she disappeared inside the depths of the bus to take her seat and wait for departure. She was gone.

Jack couldn't seem to move. Couldn't seem to do

anything more than stare at the empty air where she'd stood a few moments before.

"Come on," Layla said quietly, taking his arm.

Jack fought the urge to shake her off. He'd leave when he was damn well ready to leave and not a minute…

Mallory appeared in the doorway of the bus again, nearly knocking over a fortyish woman who was just about to board. She rushed toward Jack then hurled herself into his arms, knocking him a few steps back as he struggled to hold her and keep his balance.

"Oh God, oh God, oh God," she murmured, kissing his neck, the dampness of her tears wetting his skin. "I'm going to miss you so so much."

Jack thought he said, "Me, too," but he wasn't sure. He couldn't seem to concentrate on much of anything except the sense of completeness he felt when Mallory was in his arms.

He clamped his eyes closed and held her so tightly he was afraid she couldn't breathe. "I love you, Mall," he whispered into her ear then kissed her hair, pressing his lips tightly against her head. "Stay. Please, stay. They've caught Coco. You have a story you can run with here. You'll have money men lining up around the corner to finance your documentary now."

She pulled away from him slightly and smiled up at him, though there was no joy in the action, only sadness. "You know I can't do that," she whispered.

And in some strange, twisted way, he knew she'd refuse to stay. Knew that once she'd made her decision to leave it was a done deal. But he'd had to try one more time.

"I love you," he murmured again, kissing her ear.

"I know." She nodded, then broke away.

Jack looked up over her shoulder to find Layla wiping her cheeks and Reilly blinking rapidly.

Mallory backed away from him, her eyes big and glossy, her teeth fastened on her bottom lip. Then she smiled sadly and turned toward the bus, then disappeared for good.

15

For all intents and purposes, Mallory's life was progressing better than she would have ever imagined in Kansas City, Kansas. Within a week, she'd not only proven herself a capable producer/director of local television ads, she'd just been offered the opportunity to make a documentary on the history of the area. It would be fully funded and she'd have complete creative control.

What was strange was that none of this outer success was making her feel any better inwardly.

Oh, sure, she'd heard the saying you could never go home again. What she was finding, however, was that L.A. and Layla and Reilly and Jack had been more home to her than her hometown. No matter how many of her favorite meals her mother fixed her, no matter how many of her old friends stopped by to play catch up, her arms were raw from how often she scratched herself. She seemed to itch all over. And no matter how much lotion—calamine or otherwise—she applied, she couldn't seem to get rid of that itch.

Psoriasis, her mother told her.

You, Mallory wanted to say.

Christmas fever had hit the Midwest with a vengeance. Everywhere she looked there were blinking lights and boughs of holly, fa-la-la-la-la-la-la-la-la.

And what was with all this white stuff? How was it that she'd forgotten about how cold it could get in Kansas City in December?

She grimaced into the mirror of her white vanity. The same white vanity she had spent many a teenage morning in front of wondering who she was and where she was going.

The more things changed, the more they stayed the same.

She eyed the froufrou white four-poster twin bed done up in white eyelet lace, the academic awards her mother had framed and put up on the pink and white striped walls, and the stuffed animals that filled almost every corner of the room. No matter which house her mother lived in, or with which man, she'd always done up Mallory's room the same way, like she was expected home at any minute. It wouldn't surprise her if she came home at fifty to find the room exactly the same way. The problem always was that the room was done the way her mother thought it should look. She'd never consulted Mallory about it. If she had, the mattresses would be on the floor without a frame or a headboard, the walls would be painted a dark navy-blue and fluorescent stars would be dotted all over so that when she turned on a black light she would feel like she was sleeping outside.

She absently scratched her arm. Just being in the room made her feel full of teenage rebellion all over again.

"Are you sure you have to go to Las Vegas?" her mother said from the open door that had been closed two seconds before.

Mallory blinked at her. Lucinda was nothing if not consistent. She'd probably die wearing her Susie Homemaker aprons and crisp, striped dresses, a smile carefully affixed to her face even if it somehow never reached her eyes. Amazing that someone who'd just been married a week before couldn't muster up a real smile. Of course, it *was* her seventh marriage.

"I'm sure."

"But it's Christmas."

Mallory nodded, added the two items she'd taken from her drawer to the suitcase open on her bed. "I know. But Layla and Reilly are my best friends."

"And I'm your mother and we haven't spent Christmas together for five years. Not since you…"

The words trailed off though both of them knew where they were going. To the same place they went every time they had this discussion. What her mother had meant to say was "not since you took off to L.A. following a foolish dream that had led you right back to where you started from."

"When I get back, I'll be shopping around for my own place," she told her mother.

"No rush. You should wait until after the holidays."

And when the holidays were over her mother would tell her to wait until spring, then till after the fourth of July, then autumn, and before you knew it Mallory would be that fifty-year-old still sleeping in the twin-size canopy bed.

She shuddered.

"I'll be back the day after tomorrow," she said.

"Very well then." Far be it for her mother to argue with her.

Mallory hefted her suitcase off the bed and carried it past her mother, not stopping until she was in the foyer. She turned to find Lucinda had followed her.

"Well, I guess I'll see you the day after next," Mallory said quietly.

Her mother nodded.

Mallory faced the door, but halted before opening it. She put her suitcase on the floor then reached inside and took out the gift she'd bought for her mother. She turned to face her.

"This is for you," she said quietly. "But you're not to open it until tomorrow."

Lucinda didn't appear to know what to do as she accepted the small, neatly wrapped package.

Mallory hugged her. Really hugged her in a way

she hadn't done in a long, long time. "I'll be okay, Mom. Really, I will. I'm just going through some stuff right now that I can't share. Can't explain."

She began to suspect that all of them, all the people she passed on the street, or saw going into their houses or into work, were just wandering around trying to find their way through this maze full of broken dreams and relationships, hardships and triumphs called life.

She leaned back to smile at her mother. "When I get back, maybe I'll let you teach me how to make that jelly roll you've been bugging me about."

Lucinda nodded and smiled. This time her expression matched her eyes. "You'd better get going or you'll miss your flight."

Mallory nodded then picked up her suitcase and walked through the door feeling a little bit better about being back home.

FOUR STATES AWAY Jack sat staring at his blinking cursor, no closer to starting his monthly piece than he'd been the day before. Or the day before that. Or a week ago.

His gaze drifted to the spot where Boomer would usually be lying and quickly glanced back at the screen. Strange how you never realized how important something was until it was gone.

Ever since the day at the bus station, Layla and Reilly had been looking after him like a couple of mother hens. Considering they were both getting married tomorrow, he would have thought they'd have better things to do than bring him home-cooked meals, call him three times a day, and ply him with sticky buns. He smiled faintly. But he supposed that was what friends were for. If something like this had happened to either of them, he would like to think he'd do the same.

He clicked on the tab at the bottom of his screen, pulling up another file he'd been fooling around with.

Just Between Us—A Romantic Novel by Jack Daniels.

He stared at the words there—two entire chapters full of words—and couldn't bring himself to believe he'd written them. But after he'd stood powerlessly watching Mallory get on that damn bus for Kansas, he'd been faced with a choice of nights full of staring at the ceiling or staring at his computer and expressing his jumbled thoughts.

He'd chosen the latter.

Of course, none of this was helping him with his deadline.

He minimized the file again so that the blank screen of his article popped back up.

The phone rang in the other room.

Jack leaned back in his chair and stared at the extension, then got up and crossed to pick up the receiver on the fifth ring.

"Thank God, I caught you," his mother's voice came over the line.

Jack leaned against the wall and rubbed the pads of his index finger and thumb against his closed eyelids. "Hello, Mother."

"Look, your father and I have had a change of heart. We're reinstating your monthly stipend. You know, in the spirit of the season and all."

Jack cringed. "Thanks, but no thanks, Mother. I'm doing just fine."

Silence.

"I don't know what you're up to, Jack, but I have to say that I'm not very amused by it."

He dropped his hand to his side. "Mother, I'm thirty years old. It's long past time I cut the umbilical cord, don't you think?"

Silence again, then, "But whatever will we get you for Christmas, if we don't give you money?"

He thought about that a moment then said, "A scarf. Something blue and white, you know, to go with my jacket."

That got a laugh and he was surprised to find himself smiling.

"In L.A.?" He heard movement on her end of the phone. "Look, your father and I are in Aspen. Why don't you fly in for the holidays, Jack? We'd love to have you."

Aspen?

"I've already got plans," he said. "Don't you two ever stay home?"

Celia sighed. "That's one thing you really never understood, isn't it? That home doesn't have so much to do with a place, but the people you're with. That means if you come here, and we're here, then Aspen is home. For as long as you stay."

Her words triggered something on the outer fringes of his mind. Jack felt the urge to hang up immediately and uncover what it was.

Instead, he talked to his mother for another five minutes about the weather in Aspen, the weather in L.A., then they wished each other happy holidays then hung up the phone.

The difference was that not only did Jack feel better about the way things stood between him and his parents, but the thought ignited by his mother's innocuous words had sent adrenaline zinging through his veins.

He hurried back to the computer and started pounding out his monthly column.

MALLORY WAS NEVER ONE given to tradition and ceremony, but surely the Las Vegas wedding chapel Layla and Reilly had chosen for their double ceremony was sacrilegious. Especially considering it was Christmas Day.

Vampires?

Were these two women insane?

Yep. She was convinced that both of them had completely gone off the deep end. Had probably lost it a long time ago and she'd never really figured it out.

She glanced at the staff at Love Bite Chapel in downtown Las Vegas. They were all decked out in black and red, and wearing white makeup and sporting fangs. She suppressed a shudder even though they were likely accustomed to the reaction. In all likelihood, it was that very reaction they were after to begin with.

"Isn't this the best?" Reilly gushed as she straightened her traditional white wedding dress and grasped her blood-red roses, her hazel eyes wide as she took everything in. The ceremony would be officiated by the count himself while sitting up in an ornate maple coffin lined in red satin.

Mallory gave up trying to suppress her shudders and straight out shuddered. Yikes!

"You're surely going to burn in hell for this one," Mallory said quietly, feeling an urge to check her neck to make sure it was untouched.

Obviously something had bitten her two friends. And while it might not be the undead, the virus they'd caught had to be just as detrimental to their health. At least their mental health.

Layla joined them from the back room all decked out in her own over-the-top bridal creation that her stepmother had made her buy. She, thank goodness, looked a little more unsure than her fellow bride. The Love Bite Chapel had been a compromise. Layla had wanted Elvis to marry them while Reilly had leaned toward Liberace. They'd settled on Dracula. "You know, we may just have to go to the justice of the peace or something when we get back home. Being married by these guys... I don't know, just doesn't seem like it's real somehow."

Reilly's face looked like it was about to split in half she was smiling so widely. "Isn't it great?"

Layla and Mallory shared a glance then burst out laughing.

Who would have thought that Sugar 'n' Spice and everything very nice owner Reilly Chudowski—soon to be Reilly Kane—had such a dark streak?

"Are you ready?" a woman looking like Elvira, Mistress of the Dark, plunging neckline and silicone boobs included, asked Layla and Reilly.

Reilly nodded. Layla looked about ready to bolt for the door.

Of course, that could also be wedding jitters.

Then again, maybe not.

Six princes and princesses of the dark groomsmen and women took their places in front of the coffin, er, altar.

"You guys are insane," Mallory said aloud.

"*We're* insane?" Layla whispered to her. "I think you'd better take a long look over there before you start talking about other people's grasp on reality.''

Mallory glanced to where Layla indicated and felt every molecule of air exit her body. Sam Lovejoy and Ben Kane had taken their spots at the end of the aisle—looking none the worse for wear considering their surroundings and what was about to happen—and Jack was walking her way, looking panty-drenchingly handsome in a fitted black tux.

She hadn't seen him since getting into Vegas the night before. Yes, she had been avoiding him, but a little while ago she'd figured out that he must have been avoiding her just as much. She hadn't caught even a glimpse of him.

Until now.

He held his arm out to her. ''It's that time.''

Mallory stared into his mesmerizing brown eyes, just that minute understanding the whole attraction that vampires held. If Jack bared his teeth and showed fangs to her she would have willingly offered up her neck. Anything if he'd just be hers again.

She swallowed hard. Then again, he had never been hers, had he? Because she had refused to take him.

''Go on, you're holding things up,'' Layla said, elbowing Mallory in the back.

She stumbled forward in her too-pink taffeta bridesmaid dress that she loathed with a passion.

She had to grab a hold of Jack's offered arm to keep from tripping in her high heels.

The moment her hand made contact with his arm, she nearly cried out. It wasn't fair. It really wasn't fair that he should look so good when she looked and felt so bad.

He grinned down at her. "Are you all right?"

No. She would never be all right again.

She nodded.

Jack walked with her down the aisle then stopped when they reached the brides' side with the vampire princesses. He slowly lifted her hand and pressed his lips against the back. Mallory's thighs trembled. She'd never thought of the back of her hand as particularly sexy before, but the way he made her feel...well, he could kiss her hand anytime.

The problem was that would be hard to do while she was in Kansas and he in L.A.

She tugged her hand out of his grasp and watched as he walked to stand next to the two grooms.

Then the wedding march started.

Or, rather, the nightmare march began.

What was that music, anyway? Something from *The Munsters?* Oh, no, wait. It had been Vincent Price's theme music. Or was it something from *The Phantom of the Opera?* She grimaced, really unsure what the piece being played on the organ was, only knowing it was giving her a major case of the creeps.

Two male vampires led the brides down the aisle. Mallory glanced at Jack but he was smiling at Layla and Reilly. She caught herself scratching her bare arm and forced both her hands to her sides.

The ceremony began and Mallory thought that Layla was right. The couples would have to get married again in front of the justice of the peace. If just to make sure all this was really legal.

At the end of the ceremony when the count called for the grooms to kiss their brides, she almost couldn't keep herself from bursting out laughing. Especially when Ben dipped Reilly and nuzzled her neck as if to bite her.

Mallory met Jack's gaze over the two couples.

All those matrimonial words were still ringing in her ears: till death do us part, and we'll be together for all eternity.

And right then, Mallory knew she'd love Jack Daniels forever, no matter where she was.

16

THE JANUARY ISSUE OF *L.A. Monthly* was scheduled to hit newsstands December 30. That very day.

Jack sat at his kitchen table drinking his coffee, wondering how long he should give Mallory before he showed up on her mother's doorstep in Kansas City.

Ten author copies of the monthly periodical sat on the corner of the table, still bound. He hadn't opened them yet. Didn't need to. Because he already knew what his piece said. Word for word.

It was what might happen as a result of those words that remained up in the air.

He took a sip of coffee and grimaced when he found it cold. He couldn't seem to concentrate on much of anything lately. Not surprising, he guessed, considering that his entire future rested on the column that was in that magazine. He'd made sure that a copy of it had been overnighted to Mallory's mother's house in Kansas City with personal and confidential stamped across it.

He glanced at the other corner of his table where an open box bearing a blue and white scarf lay. He smiled as he pulled out the smooth silk and the card that lay underneath. He couldn't remember when he'd enjoyed a present from his parents more.

Yes, while his mother's words had had an impact on him, he hoped that he could have a bit of an impact on them. Rather than sending them pricey gift certificates for dinner out at the trendiest restaurants or for his mother's favorite stores in Beverly Hills, he'd instead had old photographs of them reproduced and framed. Photos of the three of them together. A family. During those few but precious times when it seemed they had been connected, these three people whose paths crossed so seldom even though they'd supposedly lived in the same house for so many years.

His mother was always harping on him to find an appropriate wife to bear her grandchildren. Anyone but Mallory, that is. But if Jack had his way, Mallory would not only be his wife, but they would have those children together. And he intended to make sure they took finger paints with them when they visited grandma, so they could smear some color on Celia's monochrome suits. And he had no doubt that his and Mallory's kids would be just the type to do something like that. They'd be unorthodox, free-spirited, with her wild hair and bright eyes and snappy intellect.

And they'd have his height and shoe size.

His brain arrested.

What was he thinking? He hadn't even won Mallory over yet and here he was giving them kids.

He propped his elbows on top of the table then rested his face against his hands. Lack of sleep had the ability to rob people of even the commonest of sense. And considering that he hadn't had any sleep since Mallory had gotten on that damn bus, well, he was surprised he was able to function at all.

He sighed and sat back in the chair. Of course, Las Vegas hadn't exactly gone down the way he'd planned it, either. Oh, she still wanted him. He could see it the instant their eyes met. Could feel it in the pit of his stomach. But he hadn't had a single opportunity to pursue that want. His time had been consumed, first, with the strange bachelor party—Sam had talked him and Ben into going to a show featuring female impersonators (the last thing Jack had been interested in after the Coco Cabana/Arnold Barr episode.) That had been quickly followed by the even stranger wedding—he swore he still smelled like garlic because he'd made sure every plate he'd eaten for the remainder of that day was loaded with garlic.

What went without saying was that he'd gone to Las Vegas knowing he had to deny his desire for her anyway. If he and Mallory had ended up together and gotten wicked in the most sinful of all cities...well, she might not take his column seriously.

And he needed her to do exactly that.

He glanced around his apartment. His nearly-empty apartment. He'd moved just about everything into storage yesterday, and the rest would go today. Everything he could pack and couldn't bear to live without—including his laptop—sat near the door. And a one-way plane ticket to Kansas City sat in front of him.

Kansas City, Here I Come.

That was the hook line of his January column. And it was exactly where he was going. Because his mother had been right. Family wasn't a place but a person. And wherever Mallory was, it was home to him. Come what may.

And if she refused him yet again?

Well, he would have to make sure she couldn't.

There was a sound outside his front door. It almost resembled a dog's bark.

His chest tightened. Boomer would have liked his decision to go after Mallory. He would have wagged his tail and looked at him with his large, watery brown eyes.

A knock.

Jack blinked. The leasing agent wasn't due for another hour yet. He glanced down at his seldom-worn watch. Maybe he'd gotten the time wrong?

He pushed from the table. He owned the place outright. But to prove to himself and Mallory that he was determined to see his decision through to the end, rather than leave the place empty, he was leasing it out. An agent was coming by to finalize the details this morning.

Another bark followed by a quiet shushing sound.

Jack grimaced as he grasped the door handle and swung the door inward. "You're early..."

But rather than staring at the leasing agent, he instead found himself looking into Mallory's much missed and exceedingly beautiful face.

Jack froze, afraid to blink in case she should disappear and leave someone else in her wake.

She smiled and he knew that the curly-haired woman wearing a T-shirt that read Power Tools—Ooooh, was indeed his Mallory.

"Hi," she said.

Jack cleared his throat then grinned. "Um, hi."

He could do little more than just stand there and stare at her.

God, she looked good. Better than anyone had a right to. And he wanted her with a ferocity that made it difficult for him to breathe.

She looked down. "I, um, just thought I'd bring my Christmas gift by," she said.

Christmas gift?

"I couldn't exactly bring her to Vegas with me. Well, if I'd had her then, anyway. But..."

Jack looked to where she was holding a red-gold puppy. A bloodhound that looked so much like Boomer the pup could have been a clone.

"It, um, took some doing, but I managed to trace Boomer's family tree. You bred him a couple of times when he was younger, remember? Before you had him neutered." She held out the pup that was all wet-brown eyes and floppy ears. "I want you to meet Boomer's granddaughter."

Jack took the pup and held her up, taking her in from the tip of her nose to the tip of her tail. It hadn't even entered his mind to get another dog. And tracing down Boomer's offspring... He held the puppy close, already feeling his heart close around the little animal. Only Mallory would be as thoughtful as this. Only Mallory would know what he was missing and would give it to him with a shrug like it was little more than telling him where the post office was. Only Mallory could move him with little or no effort at all.

"I, um, thought we could call her Junior."

Jack almost cracked up. Call a female pup Junior? He looked down at the shivering little dog and thought, why not?

Then he caught the rest of Mallory's words.

"We?" he asked, squinting at her.

It was way too early for her to have gotten a hold of a copy of *L.A. Monthly* yet. They wouldn't be on newsstands. And if she wasn't in Kansas to receive her overnighted copy...

"Aren't you going to invite me in?" she asked, sailing on by him. "Is that coffee I smell?"

Jack shook his head, closed the door and held the puppy up again to stare at her long and hard. She wagged her little tail and licked his chin. Oh, yeah. He and Junior were going to get along just fine.

He gently put her down on Boomer's old floor pillow, watching as she circled a couple of times then settled down with a soft sigh.

"Looks like she's already staking her claim," Mallory said from the doorway to the kitchen, blowing on a cup of coffee.

Just like Mallory had staked her claim on his heart three years ago.

She looked around the apartment. "Where's all your stuff?"

She didn't wait for his answer. Instead she walked around the place, peering into the empty bedroom. The only things that remained were the futon sofa where he'd slept last night, the kitchen table, a few mugs, the coffeemaker and Boomer's things, and even those he'd planned to take to storage later in the day with the help of a neighbor's truck.

Jack stared at the plane ticket to Kansas on the kitchen table then put his hand over it, sliding it from the surface then tucking it into his back pocket.

Mallory turned around and stood across the table from him. "Not very talkative this morning, are you?" She fingered the tie on the pile of magazines. "This your column?"

He nodded, his heart pounding a thousand miles a minute in his chest.

"Mallory, what are you doing here?"

She blinked at him. "I came to bring you your Christmas present, of course."

"All the way from Kansas City."

She smiled and pulled on the string to release the tie on the magazines. She picked up the top copy. "Something like that. Are you going somewhere?"

She flipped to the page at the beginning of the magazine where his piece always was, her face growing pale. She held the magazine open toward him so he could read the hook line. "Kansas City, Here I Come."

"I, um, quit my job," he said, rubbing the back of his neck. "Actually, I quit all three of my jobs."

"So you can go to Kansas?" she asked, blinking. "Why would you want to go to Kansas? You don't know anybody there."

He started at her unblinkingly. "I know you."

"But I'm not there anymore."

Jack wasn't quite following her. "Come again?"

She smiled, then walked back toward the door.

Jack knew a moment of panic. He couldn't just let her leave without explaining herself. What did she mean, she wasn't in Kansas anymore?

She opened the door and he grasped her arm. She

looked up at him, clearly puzzled. But of course Mallory would be. She could never seem to grasp how much he needed her. Never understand that he wasn't worth a damn without her in his life. Never got how much he loved her.

"Jack, let go."

His grasp slipped. She moved through the door then bent to pick something up.

Her suitcase.

She pulled it inside and put it down in the foyer.

"I hope you don't mind a new roommate," she said, smoothing the sides of her T-shirt. "We're going to have to work on the decor around here, though."

"How long?"

She stared at him. "What?"

"I asked how long? How long do you plan to stay, Mallory? Do you have some time limit? Some frame of reference? Like the one you gave yourself the first time you came to L.A.?"

She twisted her lips. "I don't know. I guess it depends on you."

She was purposely being cagey. And he wasn't sure if he wanted to take her by the shoulders and kiss her or shake her.

She cleared her throat. "Personally, I hope you'll let me stay forever."

Jack snapped straight.

Forever…

She came to stand directly in front of him, having to look up to meet his gaze. "Yes, forever," she whispered, hooking her index finger inside the waist of his jeans. "I'm not sure if that means marriage yet. Probably. But not yet. Um, Layla and Reilly's little event is still giving me nightmares, but—"

"Shut up, Mallory," Jack said, then took her face in his hands and kissed her deeply, passionately, allowing all the love he felt for her to flow freely, warming his insides.

"Oh, how I missed that," she murmured. "In fact, I missed it so much I decided I couldn't live without it. Failure or no, you've got me hooked, Jack Daniels, and I was stupid to ever think I could go on without you in my life."

Jack closed his eyes, savoring her words. It was just the response he'd been looking for with his piece. And that it hadn't taken his column for Mallory to come around meant more than anything in the world.

"Back up a minute here." She lightly bit his bottom lip. "Did you just tell me to shut up?"

He grinned and nodded. "Uh-huh."

She nibbled on his chin. "Tell me again."

"Shut up, Mallory," he whispered.

He felt her shiver then move closer to him. "Oh, I love it when you talk rough."

A tiny whine sounded around their feet. Jack

glanced down to find Junior winding around them just as another knock sounded at the door.

He kissed Mallory then reached around her to open the door to the leasing agent.

"The apartment is no longer available," he said, then slammed the door, swooped Mallory into his arms and carried her toward his bedroom.

Epilogue

Hollywood Confidential—Fifteen months later

"TONIGHT'S THE NIGHT when Hollywood puts on its shiny best and shows off its best, both in star power and product. In the best documentary feature category, I think you'll remember me mentioning one up-and-comer who has apparently arrived. Mark my words, Mallory Woodruff, oh, excuse me, now Mallory Daniels (she recently married L.A. Monthly columnist Jack Daniels whose first novel is due out next month), will walk away with this award..."

Mallory marveled at the people surrounding her and Jack in the Kodak Theater even as she scratched the sleeve of her black, sequined gown. Jack elbowed her and she stopped scratching and grinned at him. Just grinned. She was right where she'd always planned to be, sitting right here, right now, up for an award that was the papa of all awards.

More than that, she already had everything she'd always wanted without having known it was what she wanted. All that really mattered. Forget the award. Forget the documentary. She had Jack. She looked over her shoulder and squinted into the gallery. And somewhere up there Layla and Sam and Reilly and Ben sat, almost certainly as excited as she was.

"Are you okay?" Jack whispered into her ear as Billy Crystal made a crack on stage that set the audience laughing.

Mallory nodded and squeezed his hand even tighter. "I'm more than all right. I'm...perfect."

What she'd meant to say was that she felt like everything in that one moment was perfect. She was married to the man of her dreams. Her best friend, her lover, her husband. They shared a great apartment that might be short on space but long on atmosphere. And they owned a dog together that grew bigger and sweeter and even more loveable with each passing day.

She squeezed Jack's hand tighter. Still, ever since finding out she was an award nominee, memories of The Red Gardenia haunted Mallory. It wasn't so long ago, really, that Jenny Fuller had come to Hollywood to make a career for herself. And twenty-five years later, Mallory had followed in her footsteps.

The difference lay in that Jenny was dead and Mallory was happier than she'd ever been, even though the same guy that had taken Jenny's life had tried to take hers.

The same guy that was now on death row for the long-ago crime.

It took a little time to figure out that meeting Coco hadn't been the coincidence she'd thought it was. A few follow-up interviews to fill in some blanks on him had revealed that Coco had known full well who Mallory was. She had caught wind of the documentary and purposely introduced herself, her whole story about needing a place to stay a ploy to get closer so she could keep an eye on Mallory's progress. And when she got too close…

Mallory placed a hand over her stomach at the thought.

One good thing that had come out of all of this was that the police had managed to recover the money Coco had stolen. Mallory had triumphantly returned it to Layla, Reilly and Jack.

"Let's go," she whispered to Jack.

He blinked at her, surprised. "Now? They're about ready to announce the category."

She waved her hand. "Category, schmategory. I suddenly feel the tremendous urge to be alone with my husband."

Jack grinned in that sexy way that always made her toes curl up in her shoes. "Whatever Mallory wants…"

"Mallory gets," she whispered.

He got up and led the way down the row until they were rushing up the lighted aisle. Mallory ignored the curious looks they received, laughing as they burst through a set of exit doors and were thrown into almost total darkness. A dim red Exit sign was all that lighted the small hall between the theater exit and the door to the outside.

Mallory halted Jack then pressed him against the wall, staring up at him expectantly.

She couldn't believe she was doing what she was. In the other room a virtual who's who of Hollywood aristocracy was gathered and she had a small chance of appearing in front of them and waving an Oscar statue to let them know who she was. After all, it might be one of their doors she was knocking on next. And if she won that award, those doors would surely open easily.

But right now something even more monumental was on her mind. Something she couldn't contain for another moment. The news she'd planned to share with Jack right after the ceremony was just bursting to come out.

"Actually, Jack," she whispered, flattening her palm against his tuxedo shirt and sliding it teasingly downward. "I have something I want to tell you."

He craned his neck. "Shh…they're announcing the nominees."

Mallory rested her cheek against his lapel. She couldn't have cared less.

"I'm pregnant."

She heard Jack's quick intake of breath.

They'd talked about the possibility of having children often in the past few months. And while Jack's relationship with his parents was better now than it had ever been, he'd admitted he was permanently scarred by an upbringing that was void of any real demonstrations of love. A mistake he didn't want to make with his own children.

So he'd told her he wanted to have at least half a dozen and that he didn't want either of them to ever have enough money to hire a nanny.

Jack looked at her now, his gaze searching her face as if questioning whether he'd heard her right.

Mallory nodded then moved his hand to rest on her still-flat stomach. "I verified it with a doctor today. In eight months you and I are going to be the proud parents of our own living, breathing Oscar."

He hauled her closer and groaned, kissing her hair again and again. "Or Oscarette," he said, then kissed her full on the mouth.

Mallory smiled, feeling happier in that one moment than she'd ever felt in her entire life.

In the auditorium she heard an envelope being opened and the award announcer saying, "And the Oscar goes to…"

Mallory took Jack by the hand and pulled him through the door that would take them outside, already feeling more like a winner than any one person had a right to.

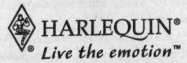

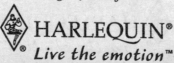

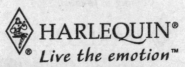

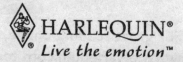

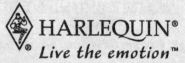

HARLEQUIN®

Temptation

THE WRONG BED

What happens when a girl finds herself in the
***wrong* bed...with the *right* guy?**

Find out in:

#866 NAUGHTY BY NATURE by Jule McBride
February 2002

#870 SOMETHING WILD by Toni Blake
March 2002

#874 CARRIED AWAY by Donna Kauffman
April 2002

#878 HER PERFECT STRANGER by Jill Shalvis
May 2002

#882 BARELY MISTAKEN by Jennifer LaBrecque
June 2002

#886 TWO TO TANGLE by Leslie Kelly
July 2002

Midnight mix-ups have never been so much fun!

HARLEQUIN®

Makes any time special ®

Visit us at www.eHarlequin.com

HTNBN2